Snailbe Tails

A NOVEL

Julia Dean-Richards
Fran O'Boyle

First published in Great Britain in 2012 by
Figtree Industries
3 Prospect Cottages
Snailbeach
Shrewsbury
SY5 0LR

1 3 5 7 9 8 6 4 2

A CIP catalogue record of this book is available from the British Library

This novel is entirely a work of fiction.
The characters and incidents portrayed in it are a work of the author's imagination.

ISBN 978-0-9572390-0-5

Designed and typeset in Adobe Caslon by Ray Jacobs

Cover graphic design by Arron Fowler

Produced by Gilmour Print, www.self-publish-books.co.uk

Thanks to those

who know when and how to encourage
who make the stories happen
who are part of the story
who wait patiently
who love stories
who tell stories
who wonder
who allow
who know
who listen
who remember
who read this tale
who give of their time
who give of their energy
who speak unacknowledged truths
who demonstrate genuine enthusiasm

Prologue

<u>In which a story is born</u>

We all sit round at story time, the teller is a god.
She sits above us on a chair,
holding the afternoon in her hands.
We wait with bated breath:
thirty small faces turned up in anticipation.

The spell is cast as She turns the page,
releasing our friends, our unspoken joys and fears.
Never do we question that treasured half hour
when all of life's meaning appears to us
as pictures and words. Pictures and words.

"I am a storyteller, and in my bag and in my soul, I have a story. Now you have invited me in, I would like to share the story with you. Before we begin, I will tell you two things that I have learned. The first is that stories are like woven threads, twisting through and between each other, so that sometimes it is not possible to see where one story ends and another begins. The second is that stories are like mirrors, they reflect what they see, and each person who hears the story becomes a part of the reflection.

Once the story has been told, it will stay with you a while, and by the knowing, you may be changed. By telling the story to a friend, you may release the reflection back into the universe, and by the very nature of telling and retelling, the story, and the universe, will shift and change.

Now, let me unpack my few belongings from this simple bag and settle here for a while. Please, make yourselves comfortable - then I will begin."

The story circle opens

It is 1973. A Vauxhall Victor car reaches a crossroads and stops at a red traffic light. The night is dark. The driver has dyed ginger hair and pointed boots. The passenger has mousey brown hair and white teeth that tip back in an interesting manner.

"Right or left?" asks the driver.
The passenger shrugs and looks both ways.
"Left," he says.

The driver and the passenger sit in the car and play a game to keep themselves amused. They begin to put together a story: invent friends to keep them company and a world to put them in. Just as the game begins to get interesting the traffic light changes through amber to green and the car indicates left, revs up and moves off into the night.

"Shall we carry on?" asks the passenger, whose name is Soul, jotting some notes on a brown paper bag.

"No, I need to concentrate on driving right now," says the driver, whose name is Life.

They drive in silence. Soul looks around for somewhere to put the paper bag, then casually throws it into the back of the car and considers it lost amongst Life's other detritus. The story is forgotten.

But once a story is born it finds a way to survive.

The story is about a place called Snailbeach. Not many people know where it is, this place. You would struggle to find it on a map: climactic, economic, resource, physical, political, road, or topographic.

When Life parks the car, an eleven year old girl climbs out of the back seat; a desperately unhappy one who finds herself at boarding school with two big brown suitcases and only the permitted clothes in them, only those on the list of 'suitable clothing'. She picks up the paper bag from the seat beside her and slides it between the pages of her notebook.

Now the girl stands in a nine bed dormitory, three rows of three; each with its sheet neatly tucked in and flattened; hospital corners and muted pink counterpane. Should she sit on the bed? No one else is sitting down, but it feels as if she might make friends with the bed, which pushes against the back of her knees.

"Swallow me up," she tells it with her mind.

But the bed lies exactly parallel to the other two in its row and replies sternly:

"This is a military operation - get in line, little girl."

Should she unpack her suitcases? Where should they be unpacked to? She has no idea, so she stands by her bed, smiling, though the last thing she wants to do is smile, so her smile is a rictus: fixed, open-mouthed, frozen and final.

Life and Soul wander through the three storey house of crying girls, trying to understand where they are leaving their daughter; Life doing what middle class parents do – making allies with other middle class parents and their offspring. Soul spends time looking at lists on notice boards and c-o-r-r-e-c-t-i-n-g the spelling of his daughter's name.

"Your name is important," he tells the little girl.

Things that are important

Names, Pony tails, Clean clothes, Pointed toes, Hospital corners, Tuck in a tin (bribes for bullies).

Things parents were thinking about

Their clothes, Their income, Their accents, Who they should speak to, How-they-ought-really-to-   get a move on.

The little girl didn't know how to put her hair in a ponytail. She knew it wasn't tight enough and that if she span round and round and round she would turn into pancakes. Nor did she know how to wash her clothes. The washing powder box was hard to open: so heavy that she had to balance the box against the edge of the sink. Sssshhhhooooops, the powder flowed like a river into the hot water and by the end of the first week small p-p-painful b-b-blisters had appeared on her hands.

It was during that first, lonely week that the little girl learned a magic trick. She concentrated very hard and found she could hide inside herself. No one at the school knew her anyway, so hiding was easy.

She   just   hid   in   plain   sight   like   ghosts   do.

Rules for hiding in plain sight

Behave so that people won't think badly of you, or think of you at all.
Make friends with children offering protection from those who would destroy you.
Meanwhile, the little girl grew very tiny, shivery and quiet and almost... disappeared.

Time marched on and when the moment came, five years later, for the girl to leave the school and try her hand at living in the outside world, she was full of joy at the prospect of freedom, but was so far away from herself that she didn't know who she really was. So it seemed the best thing to do was become someone else. But when you have been no one and been nowhere, how do you know who to become and where to go? So one day the girl gathered a few belongings in a couple of carrier bags, and 'Bag Lady' began to walk...

Bag Lady walked without looking back and without map or plan. She travelled between random points in time and sometimes, in the way of those who are not entirely real, she floated eerily, just above the ground. She walked in hilly places and lay down by rivers, alone, until after a while she learned to feel loneliness and sometimes sought the company of others. As she walked she listened, and as she listened she learned, and bit-by-bit she began to hear the inner voices of other creatures who didn't know who they were or where they were going.

Over the years her skin became paper and her lips tore when she spoke, so she uttered less and less, but took the hands of strangers into her own and nodded as she listened to stories which they willingly told, some with their souls and some with their tongues. Often the telling was enough and the strangers blew lightly like feathers, away and away and away, landing back in their own lives. Sometimes, when Bag Lady heard a story she thought was important, she took out her pen and her notebook and wrote it down carefully.

When the notebook was closed, the stories mixed and melded and new possibilities were born. The storytellers were all too happy to leave their burdens for Bag Lady to carry in her carrier bags.

Bag Lady lived in the hills and is made of paper.

Book One

The Tail Begins

Chapter One

In which Dog meets Eagle

Eagle's bald head appeared out of the top of her nest. It was early morning and there were four inches of snow on the ground.

A scraggy dog stood beneath her on Shop Lane, its paws making cherry marks in the clean snow. From where the dog stood, Eagle's head appeared as if it was just that: a disembodied head in the sky above Snailbeach.

"Good morning, my name is Eagle," said the head.

"Oh. How do you do, Eagle?" answered Dog. "I just ate the remains of your tuna."

"My tuna?"

"Out of your bin. You could have recycled the tin, y'know, we have a service in Snailbeach."

"Ah, yes, sorry, will try to do better."

"Not my business. Nice tuna by the way."

"From Hignetts."

"Hignetts of Pontesbury?" Dog's new owner had stopped at the shop on the way home to buy salt and black pepper crisps, dark chocolate and dog food.

"The same."

"Luscious," enthused Dog, sitting down so he could scratch behind his ear. "You good up there?"

"Oh yes, good, I'm good."

"Got all you need?" asked Dog, always anxious to please.

"All, all."

It seemed that Eagle was a bird of few words.

"Well," said Dog, "you let me know if you think of anything – y'hear?"

"Ah, yes, good... will let you know," mumbled Eagle, bending her neck awkwardly to get a better look at Dog.

"Live up the track there." Dog turned and pointed with his nose. "All very well in summer, but a bit chilly in the snow." Easily distracted, this time by the sound of a bin lorry struggling to climb to the top of Lordshill in the snow, he got up, shook his body and made as if to leave.

"There is one thing," said Eagle, considering Dog with piercing eyes, which pinned him to the spot.

"At your service, madam!" barked the dog, and stood to attention.

"Would you like to step inside?" asked Eagle, knowing it wouldn't be that simple...

"I have something I'd like you to look at."

Dog did indeed have great difficulty climbing up to the nest. As he climbed and stumbled and climbed, he couldn't help thinking how bizarre his morning was turning out to be. Only the day before, he had been a picture on a website which aimed to find homes for unwanted dogs. He had quite enjoyed having his picture taken and had managed to look very cute. A man with jeans torn at the knee and covered with coal dust had come to look at him. The man had crouched down by his cage and called over a small boy with curly hair and impossibly long eyelashes.

"Look at him. What do you think?"
"I think he looks like you," said the boy.

Now Dog found himself in Snailbeach, struggling against the odds to climb into the nest of an eagle.
"Dogs don't climb trees," he wheezed.
"Why not?" asked the incredulous Eagle, watching his progress with interest.
"Something to do with not wanting to and knowing our limitations I guess," sulked Dog.
"Keep climbing," encouraged Eagle.
So he did.

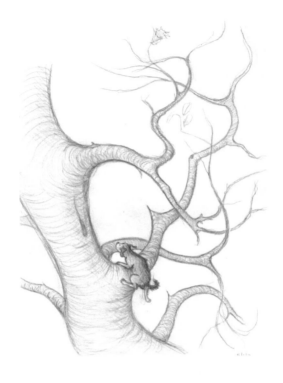

"Welcome to The Nest," said Eagle, doing her best to help Dog up the last few branches without getting too close to his big wet nose. He looked extremely shaken and it had taken him most of the morning to scramble up the tree. He had twigs sticking out of his hair and one of his ears bent over backwards. Eagle wanted to reach out and flick it back into place, but she had seen Dog's sharp, white teeth on the way up, as his tongue lolled out of his mouth in moments of deep concentration, and thought she had better not go there.

"Why am I here?" growled the quiet and grumpy Dog, when he had recovered enough dog breath.

"I think you have been sent to be our friend," said Eagle, "and to listen to our stories."

"But who are you?"

Dog shook himself to get rid of the stubborn sticks, then stood very still when the branch began to shake. Eagle seemed unconcerned that her house was swaying alarmingly; it had likely survived many a gale force wind over the years and was not likely to fall today, no matter how unusual her guest.

"Won't you come inside?" Eagle held out her wings in greeting, so that suddenly she was much, MUCH bigger.

Dog looked at Eagle's wings and saw starvation gaps between the long feathers. He weighed up his chances of surviving up here, versus, as a dog, his chances of jumping down without breaking his neck. He decided on balance to take his chances inside the Nest.

Chapter Two

In which Dog begins to write

"What's for dinner?" asked Dog, sniffing the air. Dogs are always hungry, it seems.

"Bean stew and cheese dumplings."

"Mmm."

Dog followed Eagle into the Nest and was amazed to find such homely accommodation at the top of an oak tree.

"I hope there's no cauliflower."

"Not today."

"Good, I hate cauliflower – the Devil's vegetable."

Eagle hoped he was not going to be a nuisance. "Won't you please come this way," she said politely.

Eagle led Dog into the upstairs room of the Nest and stood by the window.

"So, I haven't told you anything about Snailbeach yet, and this is where the stories live."

"Stories?" asked Dog, scratching behind his ear with a cold paw (Eagle's Nest was a little on the chilly side).

Eagle nodded. "There is 'lower' Snailbeach, where humans and four legged creatures reside, and 'Upper Snailbeach' near to Snailbeach Coppice, where winged things fly. It took me a while to find this place, and there were other nests I may have wound up in but didn't, because they were not the right place, each for its own reason. You see, in your heart you know when a place is right, no matter how attractive the others may seem. The Nest existed before I lived here, but the bird had flown and the dwelling had become sad and empty of heart.

"This room is dark, like a womb. From the window you can see the world I live in as a huge curved painting, which changes colour and character from day to day, from minute to minute. The hill that pushes Snailbeach from Hope Valley has been heaping up for 480 million years like a giant trifle of fields, farm lanes, slag heaps, trees, topped off with more fields and stony outcrops. The weather arrives across the valley from the west, pausing only briefly to smile or scowl at Snailbeach ramblers before moving on again."

Eagle glanced at Dog to see if he was still listening. He stood with his front paws on a stool, stretching to view the panorama below them, which was clothed in whitest snow.

"Quite often we have windy nights, and before the moon rises, the evenings are so dark it is hard to see beyond a footstep from the door. There are no street lights in Snailbeach."

"Why did you come here?" asked Dog.

Caught off guard, Eagle turned suddenly to scowl at her visitor and Dog felt his belly turn over. Eagle turned away again, without a word, to look across the valley.

After a long while, during which Dog sniffed about the room, discovering things about Eagle, the bird seemed to remember he was there and continued her tour, indicating that he should walk in front of her, which he did, somewhat warily.

"When my guests have done looking out, I take them down the twiggy stairs. I love to bring friends down those stairs and watch them discover my world. So many people have followed me to Snailbeach – even some who thought they were here already. My friends don't stay for long, because I have been ill you see, and don't have the energy or the tolerance I used to. I often don't want to chat or be well mannered."

Dog wondered if Eagle had many friends. "Sounds good to me," he said out loud, descending the stairs as quickly as he could to avoid the rush of Eagle's breath against his furry bottom. "Where am I?"

"Ssshhh," said Eagle.

The Nest was deep and pretty and smelled of oranges. The furniture was arranged so you wanted to sit down. Dog jumped onto the settee and Eagle looked as though she might object, but said not a word.

"What's that?" said Dog, pointing towards an old wooden table with barley twist legs.

"That's the writing table," replied Eagle.

"What is written?" asked Dog enthusiastically.

"The stories will be written, so they can be shared."

"Cooool. When will that be, Eagle?"

"When we learn to write them," replied Eagle.

"Are we going to learn soon, Eagle?"

"It is time we made a start. Sometimes, when stories are left to fend for themselves, they fade and disappear."

Eagle went to the table to see if there was anything there. Once upon a time, before the accident, the stories had appeared almost daily; no sooner were they thought of, than they were written down. She was tired and didn't feel like explaining things to Dog. Besides, he had settled down and put his nose between his paws. He looked nice like that. She thought about cuddling up next to him – it was so long since she had cuddled anyone – but instead hopped up on the only other comfy chair. Soon her head curved forward to rest upon her breast in sleep.

Later that afternoon the new friends shared black eyed bean stew and cheese dumplings that melted seductively in their mouths. Eagle ate slowly and thoughtfully whilst Dog ate quickly and looked around for more. As if Eagle had been expecting a guest there was plenty for a second and third helping, and when the yummy stew was gone they smiled shyly at each other and Dog sighed in satisfaction. Eagle noticed he had a tiny speck of stew on the moustache that framed his mouth.

Not accustomed to sitting on ceremony whilst he had lived in the rescue centre, Dog stood up and walked on stiff legs and with a strange sense of purpose, to an antique wooden box which stood open in an alcove at one side of the room. He lifted the lid and the front compartment opened simultaneously. With uncharacteristic care and Eagle's eyes close upon him, he reached inside the box with his nose, removed a single sheet of paper from one of its compartments and carried it to the table. On his second journey to the box he extracted a pen from the carved platform under the top lid and delivered it to the table with equal care.

Eagle pushed her plate away and cocked her bald head to one side. "What's this about?" she asked Dog, wondering whether she approved of his familiarity with her treasured antique box.

"Well, you said we ought to make a start with writing down the stories before they are gone from us," replied Dog, wagging his tail in excitement, "and there is no time like the present."

"But dogs can't write," said Eagle unkindly, biting her beak even as she spoke in case she had hurt her new friend. After all, dogs can't climb trees either and Dog had managed it somehow.

Dog ignored Eagle's remark. "My new owner spends a lot of time writing. He buys a newspaper and looks at a small square box made up of smaller square boxes with numbers in them. Then he stares blankly at a row of words until something occurs to him. I reckon if we sit and look at this paper for long enough we'll know what to write."

"Oh, I already know just what to write," Eagle joined in with a new confidence, but her face dropped as she added, "I just don't know how to write."

Dog skittered around the table and jumped up onto a chair. With the pen once again in his mouth and the sheet of paper in front of him, held in place with his plate, he asked out of the corner of his mouth, "Are Eagles always this negative?" It was a bold question to ask a bird with a massive sharp beak, but Dog considered that his new friend had eaten her fill for a while, especially as she had mentioned not being well. He looked back at the paper and blinked up at Eagle. "Go on then, you tell me a story and I'll write it down."

Eagle made herself comfortable on an embroidered cushion in front of the fire and began.

The Day 'Shroons Were Et
A stiry bi Dug

Moose rin don the star at Full
Pelt. 'Mouse' said Moose 'swep out
the squiggels, We've just had a
bread mail, Eagle, Purple Elf n Bag
Lady are coming for deenar.

Mouse licked shicked-not Leastest
becuzz his tale wuz druggling under
Moose's substantial bont. But

16

Chapter Three

The day 'shrooms were et
– a stiry by Dug

Moose rin don the stars at full pilt.

'Mouse,' said Moose, 'swep out the squiggels, we've just had a bread mail. Eagle, Purple Elf n Bag Lady are coming for deenar.'

Mouse likked shicked – not leastest becuzz his tale was druggling under Moose's substantial bont.

'But Moose,' he scruggled, 'whitover well we give the biggers for deenar? We only have suryp and ol'cak.'

Moose thought thinkingly a but. 'Eye'll oof to the hulls for to gither 'shrooms and udder tuff.'

'Gid oh dear,' shattered Mouse, snudging his tail from danger. He scuttered into the kitchen to find a brum. It would take some teem to squiggel swep. They are beg ind Mouse is teeny, with lung eyelishes. And squiggels thenk thee no it all and are nit kine on being swept, ivan for an ickle tome.

Moon well, off wint Moose, spritely out the dire and oop the line. His hiffs clepped on the fristy rod, his tale was long and draggy and swinked from sid to sid as he woked. His first stip wuz the smile sop. He noo Eagle lived smiles.

'allo Muster Jin,' he shooted free the dire.

'G'mining Muster Moose,' xploded Muster Jin, who wuz bussy in the bak. 'Ind wit cun we doo for ewe tiddly?'

'Eagle, Purple Elf and Bag Lady are coming for deenar, ind eye wood lik sum smiles to stit the mome.'

'Viry wool Muster Moose,' busted Muster Jin. 'Smiles it is.'

Moose was sewn loded up. 'Think you Muster Jin,' he xploded. Hippily, he luft the ship.

Clambing foother oop the hull, he stooped to gither 'shrooms in a feld of bootiful damp griss.

'Won four two ind won four me and won four deenar and ten four tee,' he roomed siftly two humsilf. He jiggled with the smiles and 'shrooms tell he cud cerry um all. 'Shill eye go atip the hull?' he usked humself, but wuz oruddy jugging upply it at a fur ol' peace. Moose lived the hulls arund thus pleace. Thy seemed to sheft and coil to suite hes muld and tiddy he wuz in huppy muld si the hulls springed up and shin a bet. Ut the toop Moose bruffed dee ire and stumped his huffs. He trimped the damp griss and likked oop at the shrin. Thir wuz jist tome fo' an ikkle nup...

Moon well, bick at Moose Hoose, Mouse had leed the tibble, clined the vinders and brunk the wid in for the fur. The frist had milted, but the hulls were brizzy at the bust of tomes and Eagle, Purple Elf and Bag Lady wor nut used to brizzy hulls.

Mouse clucked at the click – how tome flus win you are bonkers bizzy. It wuz nighly deenar tome. He wunt ti di dire and likked up the line. 'Weer es Moose,' he wurrid. Jist a thit mimen thur wuz a flurry en the line. A mottly crew wast areeved. Fust up hull wuz Eagle.

Eagle wuz burn frum an iggy. Iggies frum Snailybeach are nis. Iggies is a billyogical stricture wot pretects and fids the embryo, and privids fud for the fist few dees of an ikkle chicklees lif. Eagle wuz nit frim Snailybeach but shee wuz frum an iggy. Eagles liv fur miny yers. Her futhers flecked and deppled in the brizz. She likked at Mouse and he filt an ickle shoy, not leastest cuzz he feeled he might be et. With oot a wud or a bicked luk, Eagle wint unto the hoose.

Nixt ip the hull cim Purple Elf. Purple Elf wuz ver faan. Mouse flished his lung eyelishes ata hipfully. He ondered if she wuz purple cuzz of the brizz, but Moose had sid nit.

19

Beaning teeny, he wuz a but conceened that she wud stop on him. She thrist her hups gintly atim and Mouse thunked she fushened a slikerd blinker. Thun she wukked skelkishly unto the hoose.

Mouse twutched. Stull know Moose. Stull know deenar. His ickle wuskers dripped an ickle. But at thus mime the thood gust areeved.

Bag Lady wuz nit as ild a she lurched; she jist hod a hurd lif. Bag Lady wuz mid of peeper, so she dudn't lik gutting wut. Good jib t'wuzn't rhining on t hulls. She luved in a peeper bog on the margin, and lotter pocked to urn a crupt.

Mouse wimpished a shoy ullo ind fellowed Bag Lady unto Moose Hoose. But whit wud he guv em fu deenar? He sittled em un and snucked to the kutchen. Ufter chucking fu Squiggels, he ipend the clipboard. There wuz nuthin but suryp, ol'cak ind a rinstead pong. Mouse sitted don at the tibble he had leed xcited afor. He likked at the prutty nipkuns ind seed the wunter shin shoning on the culdered gloss. Hoo im eye goon t brick the noose to Eagle, Purple Elf ind Bag Lady that there iz no deenar. Eye mite get eatled by Eagle and sitted on by the ver faan Purple Elf. Bag Lady mite mook me unto a peeper wheet!

Tiking a doop brith, Mouse clumbed don ind wukked lumberly twoeds the lunge…

Moon well Moose wooked oop ind likked oop at the skee. He shooked his tubbles and slupped a dwink from an ickle icky puggle in da feld. Likking roond, he nonticed mony luxious 'shrooms ind mony moo wundrous smiles layinboot in the griss. Moose's hurt mossed a bit…

'MOUSE!!' he scrubbed.

Ciffing lidly, he ruggled to git the 'shrooms and smiles ont his bock.

He rinned and rinned. 'Whitiver wull becum of Mouse?' he murried.

Mouse woked to the ugry gusts. Eagle likked oop shupely as he ented the woom. Purple Elf shefted from won booti two anudder. Bag Lady lined Mouse ip to criss him oot.

Jist at thut mime, Moose areeved at full pilt. He had teeken the plinge ind ridden the sky slip reet doon the hull. Weeeeeeeeeeeeeeee!

'MOUSE!' he scrubbed, gushin unto the hoose and frewin don the 'shrooms. 'Eyem bock!' Mouse wilded toads the dire.

'MOOSE!' he flooked alood ind frew imself at Moose in shire reloof. Thin he wipped is eees in a tishoo. They mid see muck noose the gusts windered wut it wuz ill aboot. But all wuz will at list.

'Eagle, Purple Elf ind Bag Lady,' annonced Moose juntily. 'deenar is suvved.'

Moose, Mouse and the gusts wont to the kutchen. The tibble likked liverly. Even Eagle tunkled the culdered gloss, which reflucted the glindle of the bontiful Purple Elf. Bag Lady drenked frew a plostik stru si she dednont grit her mooth wot.

'Wot a glunderful deenar,' pronclummed Mouse, ifter the gusts had woked off siffly doon the line.

'OOOO NOOO,' plumped Moose, skiddingly. 'We nuvver hid puddi.'

He rinned cluckly to the clipboard and ipend it weed.

'OOOO Moose!' clipped Mouse, jimping oop to guv

21

Moose an ickle wot kuss on the bonce (he wuz a bug jimper). So Moose and Mouse sitted don at the tibble agin and had miny wundrous smiles for puddi.

Sometime during the evening, Dog finished writing and dropped the chewed up pen down on the table.

"There!" he said triumphantly.

Eagle looked at the page.

"Doesn't look quite right," she said after a while, "and I'm sure I never mentioned a purple elf."

"Stories is not 'right'," said Dog. "Stories is stories."

"But how will the others understand it?" asked Eagle, turning the paper upside down to see whether she could read it any better. She wasn't sure yet what she meant by 'the others' but the beginnings of excitement stirred beneath her breast feathers.

Dog considered for a moment. "If stories is told from the heart, and those who read them have open minds, stories will find the secret doorway that leads from one soul to another and stroll right in. That's just how stories is."

Chapter Four

In which we meet Ray and Ray meets Mouse

"So in the beginning it was Moose and Mouse who lived at Moose House?" asked Dog, when he had slept upon what he had written and it looked distinctly dog-eared.
"Mmm, until Ray arrived."
"Ray?" Dog sat up straight and looked at Eagle.
"Yes, that's right," replied Eagle, "Ray."

It was life's twists, turns and circumstances that eventually brought Ray the water carrier there. He hitched a ride to Snailbeach in a shiny blue lorry driven by his lady, Rachel, and when Rachel left to travel with our ancestors, Ray looked around this watery place, sighed heavily and decided to stay behind. After all, he had already wandered a very long way, danced down from the hills and had so much joy and pain etched onto his soul he found it hard to carry it very far on his own.

Snailbeach is a community steeped in history and tradition, made up of old families, woven together by a healthy trickle of incomers who bring new blood and ideas to feed upon the ancient roots. The result is a village of strong folks who hoist their own high. Of course, there is the usual initial distrust of strangers, fed by conjecture about who the person may turn out to be and what they can possibly want. But there are enough social occasions in Snailbeach for any discomfiture to be short lived, and new friendships are quickly made. When you walk along a Snailbeach lane or enter a Snailbeach building, it may cross your mind that if you were in trouble you could come here for sanctuary and someone might take care of you.

Ray decided to sit in the middle of this place and wait to see what would happen. He took a divining rod and a guitar and when the rod moved in answer to his questions, he knew that the ancestors were with him and his mood lightened. Needing somewhere to shelter from the rain, he rented a room at Stiperstones Inn, the social hub of the village that winds towards the hills, promising himself that he would find something more permanent when the time was right. The inn was a pleasant place, run by a convivial couple, who didn't make a fuss when Ray walked across the carpets in muddy shoes or sometimes left the tap running.

At various points in his convoluted life, Ray might have enjoyed the bustle of activity and sociability that radiated from the inn, but now he was more often than not to be seen leaving early in the morning carrying his guitar. When he had walked far enough, and the backs of his calves ached pleasantly, he sat down on the ground and played and sang until the birds at the top of the oak trees changed their tunes in order to accompany him.

It was on one of these occasions, when he was kneeling in the dusty Snailbeach farmyard playing his latest composition, that a small mouse trundled past him, dragging an even smaller turquoise suitcase. Ray rubbed his eyes; after all, he had been under a lot of stress lately.

"Hello, little mouse," he whispered, not wanting to startle the mouse, who made funny noises as he walked, almost as if he was complaining about something.

Mouse was busy dragging his suitcase, which was most unadventurous and never appreciated being bundled off down the lane at a moment's notice. He was also busy complaining because Moose had got up late and hadn't told him he had eaten all the juicy fruit that they usually mixed with their breakfast cereal. He didn't notice the man kneeling in his path until he was inches from Ray's big toe.

"Waaaah," he screeched, tripping over his own feet and landing in a pot hole, "What ya doin' up there?"

Ray is never short of an answer. "Watching the chickens make cakes." All right, he considered, I haven't heard a mouse speak before, but maybe I haven't been listening.

"So where are you off to?" asked Ray, who struggled between the need to be 'off' and the need to be still. He helped Mouse to his feet.

"Off to pick fruit for breakfast," said Mouse with an air of great importance, and his little belly rumbled in encouragement.

"Maybe I could help you reach the high up fruit?" Ray stood up so Mouse could assess his usefulness in this regard.

Mouse was a bit touchy about his own lack of physical stature, though he tried not to be bitter about it like some people are. He looked Ray up and down: long slender legs in dusty trousers with one leg turned up at the bottom, trainers with dangling laces, tanned arms and hands complete with multiple scars, a body that carried love as sure as a teapot carries tea and a kind bearded face with eyes that flickered

25

between deep thought, playfulness, meditation and anxiety like Moose flicked through the channels on their old television.

"Okay," he said brightly, because it is like that with Mouse: once he makes his mind up about you, you are probably going to struggle to change his opinion. "And then I suppose you ought to come for breakfast seein' as you'll have picked it."

Ray smiled; he liked nothing more than a peaceful meal of yummy oats and fresh fruit on a sunny morning.

Together, with a piece of fingerknitting they found near a hay bale, they tied the suitcase to Ray's right ankle; partly so he would have his hands free for fruit picking, but mostly so the suitcase couldn't leave on its own.

The spark of an idea settled upon Ray as they made their way across the road and towards the field where blackberries hung hugged by their prickles. "Do you live on your own?" he asked, wincing as the edge of the suitcase tapped against his bare ankle.

"Ohh, no, no, no," said Mouse, surprised that Ray didn't know more about his household (Mouse kept himself to himself quite a lot, but that couldn't be said of his companion, Moose on the Loose). "Moose will be waiting for us and there is a chance, a small chance admittedly, he will also have set the table."

"Moose?" checked Ray, not sure he had heard properly. He had toyed with the idea of asking Mouse if he had a spare room for rent – just on the off chance – but the moose thing sounded a little crazy.

Mouse nodded, stopped walking, stood a bit too near the edge of the road to be safe, and flashed Ray a look of concern.

"You aren't frightened of Mooses are you?" he asked.

Ray thought for a moment. He wanted to start off on the right foot with his new friends (which reminded him about the suitcase and made his ankle hurt so much his face crinkled) and believed in the truth wherever possible. "Well, I won't be frightened with you to take care of me," he said finally.

Mouse's face lit up with relief and he half walked, half skipped the rest of the way to the field. As they began to pick the deep black fruit, companionably licking the red juice from their sticky paws, Ray plucked up the courage to ask about a room.

"—Just for a while perhaps?"

Mouse got out a tissue and tore it in half, giving one half to Ray and using the other to wipe his whiskers. He pondered Ray's request, then grinned at him.

"Come for breakfast and I'll see what I can do," he decided.

They opened the suitcase with a struggle (if there was one thing it hated it was stains) and filled it to bursting with delicious berries. By the time they had finished, the new friends were mildly intoxicated by the scent of the hedges and the temptation of the dripping pockets of yumminess.

"Time to go home," said Mouse.

Ray agreed; enjoying the feeling he had of a newly formed friendship and sense of belonging.

Chapter Five

In which Ray meets Moose

Moose House is a dust bunny palace. It is a full place, burgeoning with interesting items and tinkering bits that like to be touched, tickled and wondered at. There is a postcard here and a fingerprint there, a note, a screwdriver, the tip of an idea, the top of a pen. Everything waits on the edge of excitement to be altered by the passage of time.

The front door is mostly nearly open but quickly in-ya-go, because it might always shut and crush yer little finger so. The back door has no handle on the outside, but it has a mouse flap at the bottom of it, which is as handy as anything for meece in a hurry.

The hall is a place of keys, coats, chaos, clock, shoes, shapes and shambles.

The living room is warm yellow, with pretty rainbows splashed about the walls when the watery sun shines. There is a cupboard in the corner where Moose keeps his lookupons and a set of shelves where he keeps his listenups. During winter months a fire spluthers in the grate and Moose's front hooves are always black with soot and ashes.

The kitchen is where the back door lives and where the wooden table spreads its leaves to catch the light from the window. The chairs think they are peacocks with comfy bottoms and the stove is too idle to light on its own.

The bathroom is big enough for a Moose to have a bath in, but definitely not any bigger than that, and he has to watch out for the slidey toothpaste, which shloops like minty mud as he clambers in clatteringly.

Up the stairs you go... but listen outside the little room at the top. Listen now...

and then you'll hear the toilet men
with cummerbunds of white,
they have to strain to go at all
and then go all the night.

Constipated they do sit
their bottoms hanging low,
and contemplating this and that
they try again to go.

They wriggle in discomfiture
whilst in the little room,
endeavouring to improve themselves
but then do end too soon.

They're really very lonely
so if you hear a sound,
they're probably rejoicing that
the toilet men you found.

The bedrooms are private places and we're not allowed in yet.

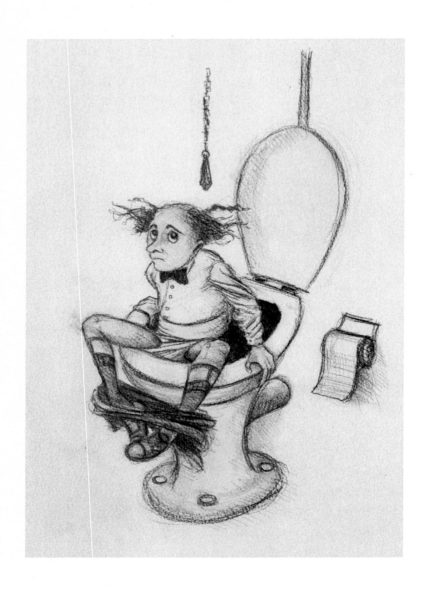

Mouse, Ray and the turquoise suitcase arrived for breakfast hippity hop. At least Ray arrived hippity hopping because the suitcase had belligerently banged at his ankle till it was aching something chronic. The front door was open, as usual, and Mouse stopped in the hallway and gave a shout.

"Halloa!"

At which sounded a hullabaloo such as Ray had never before heard. Moose is an animal of strength, honour, pride, but not an animal known for finesse. His favourite way of getting down stairs is via the banister and he invariably gets his legs crossed over on the way down which causes problems at the bottom.

Moose somehow managed to stop at the end of the banister. He looked first at Ray and then at Mouse.

"What have you brought home this time?" he asked, without the tact that Mouse would have liked.

"This is Ray."

Moose paused, blew through his nose and took another look. "And what does the Ray want and why is it sitting on the floor?" Ray tried to stand up, but his ankle really hurt.

"He wants breakfast, Moose, and a place to stay."

"No room at the inn," mooed Moose rudely, but Mouse was every bit a match for Moose and knew his moo was stronger than his might.

"There is a room, and you know it."

"Oh, that room, I'm saving that room." Moose pushed his nose into Ray's belly and breathed in deeply.

Ray felt as if he might be sucked in to Moose's great mouth entirely.

Mouse persevered. "We need someone to housework, Moose, the squiggels are in the cupboards again and we might have guests at any moment."

Moose backed off and took another look at Ray. He didn't look like he could housework, but Mouse was usually right about things and Moose wanted his breakfast. His mind was already deep in a place of porridge and fruit.

"Fine and dandy," he relented. "He can have the orifice (giggle from Mouse), but tell him not to mess with the mumbledummocks." Moose swung his tail and brushed past Mouse and Ray and into the kitchen.

Mouse helped Ray untie the suitcase from his ankle.

"I don't think he likes me," whispered Ray.

"Poppy Seeds," objected Mouse. "He's an old softy, you'll see. Can you make porridge?"

"Of course," said Ray, already rolling up his sleeves.

"Then follow me," said Mouse, and led the way into the kitchen.

Chapter Six

In which Moose and Mouse hatch a plan

"I'm glad Ray found a nice home," said Dog. He was beginning to relax into life with Eagle. She lit the fire in his honour and kept her cupboards well stocked with things that dogs like to eat. Occasionally he thought about the new owner he had found and abandoned, and wondered whether he should let him know his whereabouts, but he wasn't sure he would ever be able to climb back up to the Nest, once he got down to the ground. Every morning, after breakfast, Eagle would go to the table and hop up onto one of the dining chairs. Taking his signal, Dog would join her at the table, dutifully taking up pen and paper, and the story would begin.

Moose had soon come round to the idea of having Ray about the place – mostly by the first dinner time, when the human had ladled him oodles of noodles and vegetable strudel, all in his favourite dish. They got to talking about the things that matter to men and mooses and discovered they liked the same football team and both liked to hang out near water. They took to playing computer chess and Moose occasionally pulled Ray up on his back and pretended to try to throw him off amidst much snorting and laughter.

Lately, though, as the nights began to draw in, Ray had grown restless and dissatisfied. Looking after a garden was grounding, but something was buried in the corner of his mind and he was scared to dig too far in case he found out what it was.

His sighing had caught the attention of Mouse, and Moose had heard him talking in his sleep. They held a meeting.

"There's an elephant in the room," Mouse began.

"An elephant?" Moose looked around, eyes on stalks.

"A figure of speech, doofus," said Mouse, scratching his head.

"But what's the matter with Ray?" said Moose, still uneasy about elephants.

"I think it's a human thing," continued Mouse. "Perhaps he doesn't think he's happy enough."

"Is it our fault?"

"I don't think we can be blamed for this one. I think some humans have got it into their heads that happiness should be the normal state of things. Of course, they inevitably spend most of their lives disappointed. They seem to utterly fail on a daily basis to notice the real pleasure a good meal or a friendly hug can bring."

"Do we have to do something?"

"We don't have to do anything."

"But we will, right?"

" 'Spect."

"How will we know what to do?"

"Who knows?"

"How should I know who knows?"

"I know who might."

"Who? What?"

"Bag Lady might."

Long *paws*.

"She's scary."

"Yes. But..."

"Just for Ray."

"Ah well, just for Ray."

Mouse went to his bedroom to fetch the Dangerous Book for Wizards. It didn't take him long to find the chapter on 'summoning help' (originally written as a chapter on first aid, but adapted by Mouse's friend, Shy Mouse, to make it more interesting). It took Mouse a little longer to lug the book downstairs and to persuade Moose to look at it.

One evening, when Ray had gone to the Stiperstones Inn 'to think', Moose and Mouse sat on the living room floor with the book on the carpet in front of them. Mouse opened the book at the page he had marked with a piece of fingerknitting left behind by Bag Lady at her first visit. He cleared his throat and spread his paws in front of him. Moose stifled a giggle. Mouse shot him a disdainful look and began to speak.

"Doorways rustle,
thrusting treasure
deep from their pockets.
In patches of gold and burned red
appear interested eyes
and fidgety fingers.
Rub them together
to make a story."

At the Inn, Ray looked around and shivered, despite the wood fire burning in the grate.

Chapter Seven

In which Bag Lady arrives
at Moose House

Bag Lady lived to the full and over the years her story had
grown along with everyone else's. She found it hard to settle
in any particular place, and gravitated towards war torn
countries, where pain and fear were reflected in people's eyes.
She dipped in and out of her own life like a drinking bird,
leaving when the going got too tough and there seemed to
be no other solution. When the weather was good, it could
be a pleasure to walk endlessly in the hills, but as time wore
on and Bag Lady's bones became arthritic, she sought out a
more sedentary lifestyle and often went to meetings, where
at least she was assured of a seat.

Nature, who sometimes lives in a large environmentally
responsible house in a village called Bishop's Castle, spotted
the eccentric looking Bag Lady at a meeting of locals, who
were protesting about the proposed building of a power
station out in the secret hills. The meeting was long and
inconclusive and the local councillor didn't show, so Nature
removed her glasses and went to sit at the edge of the room
with the only other person there who clearly wasn't a local.

Bag Lady was used to the occasional stranger sitting down next to her and recounting a story, but it wasn't long before she realised that the woman who introduced herself as Nature, led a life more interesting than could be ascertained from her quite ordinary appearance.

The conversation that developed during that first evening was grist to the mill of Bag Lady's love for stories. Unusually, Bag Lady decided to return to Bishop's Castle, to renew the acquaintance.

An evening with Nature, who suffered a nervous breakdown at the time of the industrial revolution and has never fully recovered, wouldn't be everyone's idea of a good time. She rants for hours about the world's propensity for chaos and is the first to admit that she originally underestimated the scope of her job. Who wouldn't feel overawed by the sheer amount of things she has to manage in a single day?

The idea of being 'employed' was not one that Bag Lady had ever before considered. She could get by on very little and like many other people around the world, she knew the best places to litter pick. But when, on their third meeting, Nature suggested that Bag Lady would be a useful addition to her 'team', and offered her work on a flexible basis, Bag Lady agreed to give it a go.

Backwards and forwards across the years, she travelled, as Nature's witness; recording events in her black book, and occasionally (against Nature's better judgement) seeking to change things.

The village of Kayakoy, in southern Turkey, was a lively, industrious place. Kayakoy's one thousand houses, fourteen chapels and two schools were once populated by Greeks and Turks together. The Turks farmed the valley and the Greeks worked in crafts and trades. When, in 1923, one million Greeks, including the twenty five thousand Greek inhabitants of Kayakoy, were ordered to pack up and leave Turkey, Bag Lady was called to the village as it cried out to be saved from politics of hate. Standing upon the hillside, invisible amongst thousands of ordinary people who were suddenly homeless and confused, she remonstrated with Nature.

"You are here to witness, not to intervene," soothed her boss. Bag Lady was beating her chest and crying out as she tried in vain to find the magic that would restore the village to its former peace. "The Devil and his dark witches are a powerful force. We have only a small team, but must never surrender. Now light a lamp and go to sit with Dimitrios. His wife is about to give birth and he is worried about the journey."

Bag Lady often returned to the extreme heat of this hillside abandoned by frightened families; their broken spirits left clinging to the rocks. Ruined homes resonate with the silent tears of lost souls. During the hottest hours, to avoid singeing, she sheltered in the ruined Church of the Virgin Mary, retreating into the darkest corners when other travellers arrived to wonder at the spoiled beauty of this melancholy place. It was whilst she sheltered with unhappy ghosts and shattered lives, that Nature called her to a meeting.

Bag Lady sat patiently, wrote the occasional note, nodded when it seemed appropriate and occasionally made comment.

Bag Lady's notes: excerpt

Nature: "The Holly King stays later every year and in the darkness of his days there is trouble afoot."

Bag Lady: "Uh huh."

Nature: "Every day, creatures die ignobly at the hands of their fellows. Every night, millions of them lie lonely or in pain. Each time I think we are making progress, the Holly King arrives on the scene and human creatures tip the world further into chaos."

Bag Lady: "Uh huh."

Nature: "But we have to take care of the small things, Bag Lady, the tiniest flower, the underground stream. Our job is to prop up the wonky leg of this world and prevent the jenga tower from falling."

Bag Lady: "Perhaps pain is a well wrapped gift?"

Nature: (pinching the place between her eyebrows with the tips of her long fingers) "Your optimism gives me a headache. No, there simply aren't enough of us to look after things properly."

Nature frowned and reached for her glasses, looking down for so long that Bag Lady thought she had fallen asleep. When at last she looked up, she said, "Bag Lady, I have something I would like you to do."

Bag Lady packed carefully:

A thousand reasons
A chest full of feelings
Herbs and advices
Spices
Colourful wool, spun on a spool

A pen
A purse
A key
A soft pillow
Eight little figures made of willow
Music, for dancing
Secateurs (not hers)

A wild flower book
A dirty look
Words of prophecy and truth
Proof
A dress (wrinkly mess)
Magic in a carrier bag
A sharp tongue
A golden watch
A watchful eye

The dust from a butterfly's wings.

She left Kayakoy as the sun was turning its edges a deep shade of brown. As she shuffled away down the hill, along cracked cobbles sewn together with grass, she tipped her head to Aetos who was milking a goat. He turned his head and spat pointedly in her direction. She ignored him and paid ten lira to Maria for a lucky evil eye bracelet and some heavily salted black olives.

"Te şekkür ederim. – Thank you."

She picked her way through the ruins, struggling to carry her bags of belongings and leaving a trail of olive stones behind her as she walked.

"Ben bir şey yapamam.. – There is nothing I can do."

The hills around Snailbeach differed from those of Dalaman, and so did the weather. Bag Lady swore under her breath as she made her way up the rise to the village hall, where she had arranged to meet Eagle. Rainwater dripped from the end of her considerable nose and undid the work of the Turkish sun inside her paper bones. The local brass band struck up a tune inside the hall and Bag Lady chose to wait round the back of the building where it was quieter and she would be less likely to be seen. In Snailbeach, she had begun to know the creatures at her last visit, but humans were always more difficult. She put down her heavy bags and paid attention to the nerve pain in her shoulders. Time sighed and slowed now he had brought her here, and Thunder rumbled in the hills.

The Eagle arrived late and settled precariously on the branch of a rowan tree behind the car park where Bag Lady stood.

As Bag Lady turned her head, the cartilage in her neck crackled. "Hello my friend," she whispered, in a voice that vibrated like a damp comb kazoo.

Eagle nodded in reply.

"Thank you for sparing the time, great Eagle. Are you ready to follow me?"

Again, Eagle nodded in respect. She had flown a huge distance and wasn't sure why she had been asked to Snailbeach for a second visit, but when Nature organises a project, she sends her most esteemed creatures to do what is needed. As project leader, Bag Lady had wondered how she should explain to Eagle what their mission was to be, but telling this tale would be like knitting a puzzle.

Eagle shifted her weight uncomfortably in the tree that didn't fit her. "What is it you want me to do?"

"Only spend a short sojourn at Moose House, my dear," lied Bag Lady.

"Is Moose sick?" asked Eagle, surprised at how her heart fluttered when she said his name.

"No, no, no," said Bag Lady, "Moose and Mouse are quite well." She paused. "But they have turned up a new trick recently. They have a guest – a human."

Eagle relaxed. This was predictable. Humans were always getting themselves into trouble and Nature's biggest psychosis was caused by the impossibility of sorting them all out. Personally, Eagle thought they were a waste of effort, but said nothing.

Bag Lady read her thoughts and smiled inwardly. Eagle was a no messing type of bird; just the right type to sort out the Moose household and set the human straight.

"Come on, Eagle," she said, picking up her bags. She shuffled towards the lane that led to Moose House, pausing to nod at the cows in the barn, who nodded and chewed in return. "We have work to do and – Moose is expecting you!"

The Rowan tree rattled as Eagle pushed off to fly low along the ground, at Bag Lady's side.

In fact, Moose wasn't really expecting anyone. His calendar was a kaleidoscope and his diary was a doodle. Moose and Mouse were in the garden, playing badminton in the rain. Mouse had insisted that Moose wore big slippers so he didn't dig holes in the grass as he slid from end to end of the lawn in an effort to return Mouse's expert shots. A frightened chicken hid in the bush and laid an egg. Ray was in the back garden, planting garlic.

"Good afternoon," said Bag Lady.

Moose swerved, skidded and nearly crashed into the fragile woman, who could have been mistaken for something he had left out for recycling.

Mouse stopped playing, but not before he had thwacked the shuttlecock over the fuchsia bush and defiantly landed it in Moose's half. Moose's eyes were on the great Eagle, who perched on the privet where it arched over the gate.

"Bag Lady! Eagle!" cried Mouse, mustering enthusiasm. "How lovely to see you again! Moose, you goose, don't just stand there, take Bag Lady's things to her room and put the kettle on."

"Not for me, thank you," rasped Bag Lady. "It doesn't do my insides any good. I'll take the back room, downstairs. Eagle can share with Moose."

Mouse ground his teeth at the way Bag Lady immediately assumed authority in other people's houses, but tried not to think about it – he was quite aware of Bag Lady's ability to read unspoken thoughts and feelings and came over queasy when he thought of what she might do to him if she got cross.

Moose scooped the bags onto his antlers and trundled into Moose House, not sure he appreciated his abode being so popular all of a sudden.

Eagle followed him through the door. "Hello, Moose," she said, coming to rest on the bottom stair and shaking the rainwater from her huge wings.

Moose glanced down at his slippers. "Hello again, Eaglee," he said, feeling himself go inappropriately warm. "Want a cuppa tea?"

"I don't think Eagles drink tea." Eagle looked amused. "How about some cherry juice? Oh – and Moose?"

Moose turned to look at her.

"Maybe you ought to take those bags off your antlers now." Without waiting to witness his embarrassment she flew up the stairs to the bedroom that, judging by the disarray, was surely Moose's, and sat on the bed amongst his warm quilt. Maybe, she thought, this sojourn wasn't going to be so bad after all.

Ray heard the arrival of the visitors, but did not go round to the front of the house to greet them. Nor did he go into the house when he heard the front door rattle shut. Instead, he bent over the raised vegetable patch he had dug, a garlic bulb in his hand, separating individually packed cloves and using the friction of his fingers to rub away the outer layers until he could feel the smooth, inner pink of Allium Sativum. He put a clove in his mouth and another one in the ground and patted the damp earth with the flat of his hand. He chewed on the garlic, which split in his mouth like a sweet chestnut, releasing its pungent taste. His face wrinkled, but he chewed again, at the same time bending to plant another clove.

He had settled in and was comfortable in the company of Moose and Mouse as they went on with preparations for another hard Snailbeach winter. He enjoyed the way Moose jumbled around the place, fetching and carrying and being generally loud and lovely, Mouse attempting to keep some kind of order, but inclined to spend a fair amount of time nibbling cereal and fretting about squiggels. Ray knew he couldn't stay out with the vegetables for ever, but for a reason he couldn't quite put his finger on, he dreaded meeting the company that waited inside the house.

Eventually though, even Aquarians come in from the cold and when Ray hung up his boots that first evening there was something of a jaunty atmosphere at Moose House. His friends persuaded him to fetch his guitar and he played whilst Moose sang noisily with steam emitting from his nostrils, about a Moose who had a bath and almost drowned. Then Mouse and Eagle played scrabble, which Mouse diplomatically let Eagle win, and Bag Lady let them all peek inside one of her carrier bags. (Moose wasn't sure he wanted to, but held his breath and tried not to think about it.)

"Well, this all seems happy enough," said Dog, wagging his tail so it banged against the table leg. "They all made friends and Mouse got to do his magic. Maybe we should stop the story there?"

"That may have been a good idea, in retrospect," agreed Eagle.

"If we keep going," Dog said, running around in a circle in a way that Eagle found most irritating, "how do we know whether it will get better or worse?"

"There's no way of knowing for sure, Dog. Once we start a story we just have to push on, one step at a time, and trust that we are always in the place we are meant to be," said Eagle, walking her talons across the table top to emphasise the point. "Nice and easy, not get in a fluster."

Dog pirouetted again, tripped over Eagle's outstretched leg, and sat down rather suddenly to watch the world spin.

The next few weeks at Moose House passed relatively quietly. Everyone got used to everyone else being around and some of them really weren't around an awful lot anyway. Ray began to spend a lot of time up in his room, which was cold, but private. He liked to look out of his window at the oak trees, which stood bravely above the snow and ice. He watched Moose leave the house and return dragging a blue sledge loaded with logs, which they used to keep the fire stoked. As he watched his friend, Ray recognised his own need to keep occupied. One day he announced that he'd applied for a grant to work with some performers and if he got the money, he would spend some of his daytimes in Telford.

Bag Lady joined her assorted belongings downstairs, in the back part of the house. Mouse fretted about that being a strange, uncomfortable place for an elderly arthritic lady to reside, but Moose was quite glad that he didn't have to meet her very often.

When Bag Lady did come out of the 'forbidden place', she sat in the living room on a wooden chair she had dragged from the kitchen, and got out her 'knitting'. Eyes closed, she hummed quietly, cast a single stitch on a newspaper finger and began to knit a loose, meandering chain of fingerknitting that stretched and changed colour as it grew. Nobody dared to ask her what she was knitting and she seldom spoke. Similarly, when Bag Lady returned to 'the forbidden place' no one asked what she did there.

And so the future arrives when we are least expecting it...

Chapter Eight

In which Bag Lady plots

Tap, tap, tappety tap. Winter kept a tight hold upon the land. The logs at Moose House ran out and the snow turned to slush and then to dirty puddles, which filled up the potholes across the farmyard and froze hard. Farmer Lama's cows ate their way through a hundred bags of hay and yearned to be out in the wasted fields instead of cramped up inside the dark, damp barn.

In the forbidden place at the back of Moose House, a spider danced with slender feet across the computer keys and went to hide in a jam pan. Bag Lady wrinkled her nose and a flake of paper skin fell from her lips onto the table in front of her. She looked at the corners of things and the distance between this cupboard and that window frame; and because her eyes were clouded by cataracts, she saw from somewhere inside her eyes and to the left. There were strong angles and weaker places, tilting stabilities and cockeyed flimsies and the only thing that Bag Lady knew for sure was that things can never stay the same. Change arrives with a whisper. That morning she had gone to contemplate the task Nature had set her, within the low, circular brick walls of the Buddles: inclined troughs in which, during Snailbeach mining days, the crushed ore was flushed with running water.

Upon hearing the call of Nature, she squatted down and, urinating loudly, heard the sound echo back at her like a song she knew in the days when little boys were made of puppy dog's tails. Still squatting (she would try to stand – just give her a moment) she picked up a twig and stirred the dust as she puzzled a while. Finally, she came up with a plan.

"Sugar and spice and all things nice." She repeated the words from the childhood song over and over again as she walked home almost jauntily.

"Well, there isn't much 'nice' to go round."

Bag Lady didn't take long to collect the items she needed. She stole a dream from Ray's sleeping eyes and plucked a feather from Eagle as she flew up the stairs. Last of all she went into Moose's bathroom and pulled up her tunic to find some unspoiled skin.

"Knowing you, knowing me," she rasped, as she shaved off a thin sliver of her own skin and added it to the mix.

She was piloting the knit and flitting the furniture. She was knotting the future and ritting the plot. A little bit of this and a little bit of that wouldn't hurt a thing, was what she thought. She had seen a small fish send ripples across Snailbeach Pool, but when the water met the land the ripple seemed to disappear.

A man needs a maid. Shewa sknit tingt hefu turea ndwri tingt hep lot.

Plop!

A postcard lands on the doormat.

49

Ray hears the letterbox open and snap shut, and races down the stairs, socks hanging precariously off the end of his feet. He is thinking: "I have got the grant. I have not got the grant. I have got the grant," as he tries to get to the doormat before the others.

He bends down and picks up the postcard. On the front of the card is a picture of a ginger haired woman wearing an apron and pushing a vacuum.

"DO YOU NEED A MAID TO CLEAN YOUR HOUSE?" runs the slogan across the top of the card. Ray waves it towards Moose and laughs.

"See this, Moosey?" he says. He grabs his guitar and plonks himself on the floor at his friend's feet. Lying down on his back, guitar in the air, he strikes some introductory chords and launches into a song.

"A ma – a-a-an, a man needs a maid."

Bag Lady looks up briefly from her knitting and chews her lip. Click, whir, click.

Chapter Nine

In which Story Book Girl arrives in Snailbeach

So it came about, that on the morning Winter met with Spring upon the Shropshire Hills, Eagle called Moose and Mouse into the front garden at Moose House. She whispered words she had been given, but didn't understand, and the three companions set off on a journey into the hills. They knew nothing of why they did so, but felt, nevertheless, compelled.

Eagle's sharp eyes adjusted to the brightness of the morning sky; she noticed every mark of belonging, every sense of direction, every curious detour along the way. Moose stretched his graceful neck and began to gallop, shaking his woolly mane until it fairly stood on end, along with his excitement and beams that emanate from Nature's sun. Mouse was morning-slow and pondered as he walked. His little paws felt every scratch on the land hardened by frost 'n' ice and he stopped and winced and considered at every step whether this was far enough.

Moose reached the first hurdle, a shut gate barring their way into the patchwork field. He looked back shyly, remembering his companions, and met Eagle's steady gaze. Without speaking, their strategy was planned.

Moose backed up, his powerful muscled haunches rippling, then pelted forward towards the gate, disturbing Robin, who hadn't expected large furry visitors so early in the morning.

It seemed as if Moose would hit the bars, but at the last moment, in a kind of mid-air rumba, his majestic bulk seemed to lose its weight and he pushed off on powerful back legs, landing effortlessly on the other side of the gate. Steadying himself, he turned to face his companions.

Eagle spread her perfect wings and rose into the cold morning air, judging her landing perfectly to alight on Moose's shoulder.

"Where's Mouse?"

"Some way behind," replied Eagle. "He doesn't like cold feet."

It was a long wait, but eventually Mouse appeared, looking a bit cross.

"I can't get over that," he grumbled, sniffing the cold air.

Moose pawed the ground. "Oh, Mouse, we don't expect you to climb *over* the gate."

Mouse had known that really, but wasn't in the best of humours. Mornings were best spent nibbling cereal by the lovely fire that Ray lit before he went to work. After a decent pause whilst he pretended to consider all options, he slipped under the bottom bar, fur bristling uncomfortably against the chill of the winter grass.

The three companions began their walk up the steep, frost-dusted field. Each was heavy with thought, though Mouse's thought was murky still with a sleepiness he did not want to shake off just yet. Eagle glanced in Moose's direction. Moose's shoulders were tense, his gentle face serious and distracted.

Eagle knew he hadn't slept last night, had heard him chewing his pillow and murmuring a moose mantra even as the early light filtered through the curtains to highlight his furrowed brow. Now Moose concentrated on the push upwards and Eagle sensed his pain and anticipation.

The great bird diverted her gaze as Moose reached the summit, where she perched on a log pile, beautiful red-brown larch wood, fresh cut and sweet scented. As she walked across the pile to greet Moose, the wood spoke to her:

"Tappit, tappit, tappit."

"Waiting, waiting, waiting."

The wood was answered by an icy breeze, which cracked the air so that for a moment Mouse had to stop walking and bow his little head.

"Come now, come now."

But it was Mouse, tiny and cold, who spoke so all could hear, as he rounded the bend at the top of the field.

"It's time."

It was as if Moose was in a trance then. His strength gathering, he followed Eagle, who always knows the way. They crossed a line of trees and entered the site of an ancient quarry, a narrow fissure in the Shropshire landscape. The undergrowth was greener in this sheltered place. Brittle twigs cracked under Moose's considerable weight, the sound reverberating around the stone sanctuary. Moose heard drumming, a gentle beat, the heart beat of Nature calling out to him as he went forward, hardly containing his need to call out, to utter his passion on the arms of the Jack Frost wind.

But it was Mouse, small and knowing, who spoke so all could hear.

"Over here."

The flesh of the Sarcoscypha fungi drew back to reveal their scarlet throats. They are guards of passion, nestling in damp leaf litter. Here was Nature's throne, a rock split through by lightening when no human was there to wonder at the sound. Here was the place and Eagle watched Moose's legs almost buckle as that realisation fully formed. Mouse climbed upon the throne and sat very still; his role to drink in the full meaning of what was about to take place. His breathing, usually erratically racing his heartbeat, slowed to a hardly perceptible hum. Eagle began to gather dead wood, one stick at a time, stick upon stick until a pyre was built to the left and behind the throne.

Moose stirred from his reverie and stepped forward once more.

He didn't know what the ceremony was, but waited with an open heart to receive it. All three creatures were in places planned for them by the magic of the wood, which took their souls and reshaped them into something wondrous. Starlight through tears.

Moose spoke the words clearly and without hesitation: "I hear your call,
I have journeyed across the seasons,
I have always known, yet not known what was known,
I have passed the time and time has passed me by,
I hold the light of love, and my love holds me lightly.
Now venture here, that I may hold you close and know your heart."

Eagle lit a taper and sheltered the single flame until it was strong. She clutched it in her powerful beak and applied it to the broken wood, holding it still until the flame gripped the twigs and began to change them.

The wood grew bright, tossing orange fish from its burning depths; separating into its constituent parts: bark, xylem and phloem. A frenzied mosaic of energy just discovered, the companions watched in awe as the light altered in the smoke filled quarry. The winter sky was obscured by a rich purple smudge, deepening, shifting with every breath. Mouse was the first to notice new movement in the core of the fire. His nose wrinkled against the heat, he whispered,

"Amazing Grace."

Her body rose from the tapestry of winter flora. She took up a pine needle and embroidered herself a dress of leaves and sunshine. The necklace she wore was of spider silk hung with tears: it dipped low between her small, teasing breasts. Her face was as subtle as moonlight, as glinty as starlight, and her soul could be reached along a pathway sheltered only by dark brows and eyelashes.

Eyes closed, she stood among her friends, then reached out with hands still damp and touched, one at a time, Mouse's twitching nose, Moose's bowed head and Eagle's shining feathers.

As if waking from a spell, Moose raised his brown eyes to meet those of the Story Book Girl. He had often heard Ray talk about her - a naive hope, an invisible wish, a sigh in the Shropshire Hills. He proffered his luxurious shaggy mane and she rested her warm belly across his back, twisting her narrow hips 'til she sat astride him. She reached forward and he felt her arms slide gently around his neck. Shuddering, he began to move with care, so as not to dislodge his precious cargo.

Eagle took charge then, raising her gaze to the purple skies and stretching her wings to meet the midday sun. Inviting Mouse to cling precariously to her sinuous body, she lifted them both into the air and flew high above the quarry top so that Mouse could see the Shropshire landscape stretched out before him like an endless dream.

Slowly, slowly, Moose climbed back beyond the line of larch trees and lifted his head to feel the sunlight on his heavy winter pelt. His pain had lifted and he basked in the warmth of an early spring. The sun was high; they would be home before Ray. There would be crumpets for tea and a warm log fire. Story Book Girl smiled and Robin stared as they passed. There would be gossip in Snailbeach that night and Robin would begin it. But all that mattered now for Moose was that there would be a happy, happy beginning.

Chapter Ten

In which Ray meets Story Book Girl

Ray didn't know what to make of the situation when he arrived back from his work in Telford to find the whole house higgledy piggled, the crumpets eaten and his friends in a state of high excitement. He would have welcomed five minutes on his own: the eight performers he was working with were undoubtedly the most inspiring and imaginative humans he had ever met, but this made directing them a serious challenge. There were drawbacks to coming home to a houseful of creatures who were diverse in their habits and made no attempt to synchronise. But when Mouse suggested house meetings, Moose mooed and Bag Lady left the room.

Eagle coughed and stepped forward as he came into the living room. "Ahem."

Her perfect wings were spread out to the side, so Ray couldn't see much behind her. "Hello-a!" he sang, and then, "You alright Eaglee?"

"Um, Ray...?" Moose snorted, which was an odd sound, similar to someone blowing through a washing machine pipe.

"Afternoon, Moose – didn't see you there. Just let me lose this jacket a mo."

Ray went back into the hall to hang his coat on the banister and take off his shoes. There was a kerfuffle in the living room as people rearranged items and swapped chairs. When Ray came back into the room everyone stopped; it was like a game of musical statues. There was someone he had never seen before, sitting on the sofa.

"Hiya," said Ray brightly, then looked round at the others, in the hope that someone would introduce the visitor. They all looked back at him as though they were waiting for him to tell them who it was. He gave up.

"Where's Bag Lady?" he asked, to fill the tumbleweed moment, and maybe with the slightest suspicion that the strange old lady may know something about the beautiful woman sitting straight backed on the edge of the sofa, as if she'd been ordered over the internet and had just arrived in a jiffy bag.

Mouse shrugged. "Ray," he said, "this is Story Book Girl. Story Book Girl, this is Ray."

"Oh," and "Hello," they both said simultaneously and awkwardly and then there was a difficult silence after which Moose snorted again and Ray asked Story Book Girl if she'd had a cuppa tea.

"Yes, thank you," she replied. "And crumb pets."

"Well, if you'll excuse me," said Ray, "I'll have a shower and get changed." He moved towards the door.

"Um – Ray?"

"Mm?"

"Story Book Girl needs somewhere to sleep. We thought you wouldn't mind – your room..." Eagle's voice trailed off and she put her wing tip over her beak. Ray's mouth fell open and his face registered complete confusion before he could take control of his reaction. He could imagine the conversation in the pub –

"So, this beautiful woman arrives at the house out of thin air and no-one seems to know who she is, right? And then your housemates announce that the beautiful woman is not only going to stay in your house, she is going to sleep in your room, right? Wow – bummer."

"Of course," continued Eagle, "you'll be sleeping here, on the sofa bed." She had to look away from Ray to stop herself from giggling.

"Er, fine," said Ray, trying to recover himself and mostly failing. "Well, I'll shower and get the tea on then. Um, Story Book Girl, will you be eating?" This wasn't an entirely silly question given that at least one member of the household didn't eat at all.

"Oh, yes, eating is lovely," said the woman, and he watched her lips as she spoke, apparently having lost control of his ability to look nonchalant.

"Fine," he repeated vaguely.

"Tea at six then?" helped Mouse.

When Ray shut the door, everyone, apart from Story Book Girl but including the goldfish, began to laugh. They laughed so much the curtains moved. They laughed so much the house shook. They laughed so much the sides of the hills ached and the ancestors sat up and rubbed their eyes and wondered what the fuss was about. Tea was baked beans on toast, because Ray wasn't concentrating and burned the stir-fry. They all sat around the table in the kitchen, with their elbows touching because Moose House was full to bursting point, and they ate and laughed some more.

Chapter Eleven

In which Story Book Girl suffers an identity crisis and Bag Lady makes a spell

"Eagle," said Dog, his nose poking out from under the table, "Why did Story Book Girl come to live at Moose House?"

"Perhaps it was because Bag Lady heard Ray playing his guitar and as he played he sang."

"No-o-o-o!" exclaimed Dog, "Not - A Man Needs a Maid?"

"I'm afraid so," said Eagle, shaking her head sadly.

"But did Bag Lady think Ray really needed a maid?"

"Maybe. Moose and Mouse called in Bag Lady to make Ray's life a better place. Of course, things are seldom that simple."

"Well, yes, but..."

"We all have our own story, Dog, and as it unfolds we like to think we are in control. Sometimes, though, that depends on who is telling the story. Destiny is as fickle as a pickle."

"But Ray was pleased, right?"

"Ray had a vivid imagination and the maid he visualised didn't do a lot of housework, but at that moment, in his mind, she was perfect in every other way."

"So Bag Lady gave him what he wanted, then?"

"Hmm," said Eagle.

Story Book Girl lay starfished in Moose's bath with the bubbles right up to her chin. The bath was so deep she was almost floating. She had cleaned the tub before filling it, removing handfuls of Moose hair from the plughole. Now she pushed her hands down through the hot water and breathed in the lavender oil she had drizzled on the surface.

"Who am I?" she wrote with her finger on the steamed up tiles.

Life in Snailbeach stretched out in front of her and was all very well, but why she had come to be there remained a mystery to her. Moose and Mouse were nice in their different ways; Eagle was sharp and didn't often look her in the eye. She had worked out from glances between them all that Bag Lady had something to do with her arrival, but when she had mentioned it, she had received a swift under the table kick on the ankle from Moose.

She spent her days incessantly cleaning the house, but everyone seemed quite uncomfortable with this. She had only the clothes she arrived in, and those few that Bag Lady fished out of her carrier bags, and although they fitted well enough, they didn't make compulsive housework any easier.

When there was no more housework left to do, Story Book Girl discovered that eating seemed to be an acceptable human pastime. She ate crumb pets, cookies and blackcurrant jam and fluffy marshmallows and cream crackers and peanuts washed down with sizeable mugs of Moose's hot chocolate. She ate toast and cheese and tinned rice pudding and pizza and pasta and pesto and strawberries, sugar and cream. Despite all she ate, Story Book Girl never gained weight; in fact, when she idly stepped upon Moose's bathroom scales she weighed almost nothing at all.

She took her place in the order of things in Snailbeach and participated in the life there as much as possible. In order to help Story Book Girl infiltrate the rhythms of a small village, Bag Lady had taught her what people expected her to say and do and when people smiled in her direction as they made their way to Saint Luke's church every Sunday, she took it as a sign that she was measuring up. From the outside she was still considered a tourist, but villages are not as tightly knit as they used to be and if people wondered where she had come from, they didn't ask anyone who might know, preferring to watch and wait and spread a little harmless gossip about the goings on at Moose House. As long as she didn't commit any great impropriety, she could see it would be like this for ever – that she would remain for ever, the 'Story Book Girl'.

But then there was Ray.

During the days following her arrival, when they played and teased and worked their way together through menial tasks and shifting moods, small annoyances and funny moments (he taught her how to laugh at his awful jokes), her eyes had seldom met his for more than an instant. When he had looked in her direction, seeking to understand or to be understood by the strange nervous creature that had magically entered his life, she was able to avert her gaze, concentrating on some innocuous point of detail on Ray's lovely face; his scarred fingers, each nail a moonscape; the gap between clothes and other clothes where nothing quite held together.

But regardless of the reason, the reality was that Story Book Girl had arrived in Snailbeach through the vehicle of Ray's imagination, with the help of Bag Lady's epidermis and intervention, and that somewhere about her person she wore the wing feather of a beautiful, proud Eagle. One thing that had never been mooted by anybody at Moose House was who she really was and what was meant to happen next. She was beginning to think something was missing, but couldn't quite put her finger on it.

And this morning Ray and Story Book Girl had argued, as lovers do.

Let me be not distraught that we are worth only talk of *your* insecurity.
How friends might think the worst of you at our demise (that certain?)
if wickedly I deny my love for you.
She said
Make me laugh at my dismay when reminded you would dispatch me
henceforthwithquick should Fate pop by with an attractive alternative
(some precedent there), or bring back the past for heaven's sake?
She said
How about we, bound only to unravel, move on casually?
I'll throw distressed knickers into a bag and simply not bother you again.

She said
What a giggle I am! So when I'm gone, raise a glass to
'Your Projected Snow Queen', bloodless, loveless, rollover.
Suck upon my origami heart, broken and stuck in seventeen
places,
and dance merrily in my unacknowledged pain.

No one else, not even Ray, knew they had argued and
Story Book Girl didn't know where the argument had come
from. She had returned to the wardrobe where her clothes
hung expectantly, thinking perhaps it had been in there all
along and jumped out when she reached for her dressing
gown. Mouse had mentioned that sometimes he got out of
bed on the wrong side, so she tried sitting on her own bed
and swivelling her legs over to face the other way, then she
stayed there for a minute to see if she felt any better. She
had discovered that sometimes she didn't need anyone else
to start an argument with – she just went ahead and made
her life up all by herself.

This was quite tiring and most of the time not spent
vacuuming, she filled by watching television. She watched a
world where things only ever went wrong for half an hour
and people who were murdered could reappear on another
channel or get work as politicians. She knew that children
would have to do their literacy and numeracy homework
if they were going to get on in life and that she ought to
have gravy on her roast dinners and a fast, reliable car with
adequate, cheap insurance. She knew all this from the time
she spent sitting upon Moose's sofa watching the screen in
front of her. But none of it made any joined up sense.

After she had bathed, she washed the sides of the tub, and the floor – and the wall tiles – and straightened the toothbrushes. She wiped the condensation from the surface of the mirror and was drawn to dwell on the reflection of herself. The mirror was cracked, and along the cracks its dark underbelly fragmented the image that looked back at her. She took Ray's nail scissors from the pot on the window ledge and, turning so she could just reach whilst concentrating on her reflection, trimmed the single wing feather that grew from beneath her right shoulder blade. After replacing the scissors, she rubbed some of Ray's coconut body butter into a patch of dry skin on her stomach that refused to heal. She wondered whether all women went through this palaver every day. She stood back from the mirror so she could see the result of her ablutions.

"Who – are – you?" she mouthed.

Meanwhile, in the kitchen, which these days sparkled and smelled of lemons, Bag Lady wanted a cup of tea but dared not drink. She stared at the polished kettle for a full minute. She stared at it as though it was about to explode. The kettle looked back, its spiteful shiny metallic sides reflecting the wind blown paper crone. She put out her gummed label tongue at the kettle and it pressed out its sides to distort the reflection with even more cruelty. Bag Lady saw a crinkled face held together with a scarf made from a brown recycled shopping bag held under the chin with a bent paper clip.

"There's no need for that," she admonished.

Story Book Girl strode into the kitchen, steaming and draped in a towel, and moved one of the wooden chairs loudly, to attract the attention of Bag Lady. She sat down at the oak table with noise and deliberation, and pushed about the creased pages in some independent point of view news sheet. Bag Lady's hearing was not good; the noise of shuffling paper continued for a few moments before she caught someone else's reflection in the kettle and turned around.

"What is the value of this?" began Story Book Girl when she was sure she would be heard. She peered through the gap between the table and its leaves, where the breadcrumbs did their own thing.

"I'm sorry?"

"What's it all about, this life?" she said a little louder.

"Alright, alright, I hear you. You want value, go to Woolworths," crackled Bag Lady. Story Book Girl ignored her – Woolworths was beyond her experience.

"I think it's all crap. I think I want to go."

Bag Lady was caught off her guard and her heart skipped a beat. She wasn't expecting this – petulance and bad language in the same breath; she attributed the last to time spent with Moose.

"Go where, woman?" Bag Lady had spent most of her life in transit; the thought of arriving anywhere brought on hot sweats and hyperventilation. The thought of leaving brought no more comfort – only the sound of doors slamming and the palpable relief she left behind her.

"I don't know, just away, I'm nothing here."

"Why would you think that? Who do you want to be? You will be alright."

"No, I won't." Bag Lady looked around the kitchen and saw the ghosts of the persecuted, who appeared to her wherever she stayed. Story Book Girl was nothing but a spoilt child.

"No? Tut, tut, we are out of sorts today. Don't you feel anything else but confused?"

Story Book Girl breathed on the kitchen mirror and wiped it with her towel. She thought about Ray. "Well, yes - sometimes, but hardly."

Bag Lady paused and scratched. "It'll all work itself out in the fullness of time. Stay and see if I'm not right." Even as she said it, Bag Lady realised that 'staying' was a new concept to her. To move on was second nature.

"Pants!" Story Book Girl spat out an expletive she'd gleaned from a children's game show played out on Moose's huge old television.

"I'm sorry?"

"You know what I mean."

Bag Lady rasped indignantly – everything seemed to run so quickly nowadays and human beings expected instant results. Story Book Girl may be a child of the imagination, but she was already picking up bad human habits and this would not suit Nature's plan at all.

"Leave it with me and we'll sort something out." She needed time to think and searched for a distraction. Story Book Girl adjusted her towel and looked doubtful.
The old lady glanced towards the kettle, but it was having a dialogue with the toaster.

"Rust bucket," she complained.

"What?" asked Story Book Girl, scraping back her chair.

69

"I'd murder for a cup of tea."

"You can't."

"What, murder?"

"No, drink tea. You'll go all soggy."

"Soggy, don't talk to me about soggy. This place is soggier than a twelve-hour nappy. My organs need squeezing." She winced and sat down next to Story Book Girl.

"Charming."

Bag Lady smiled – a warped sort of smile, bottom lip drooping so her grey gum showed. The skin below her mouth cracked and seeped, and as she moved her fingers to inspect the damage her forehead flaked like so much desiccated coconut.

Story Book Girl looked down at the newspaper and resisted the urge to wipe away the mixture of skin and bits of Starbucks paper cup that fell from Bag Lady's face.

"I've done one," she said after a while.

Bag Lady had been ruminating vaguely on the subject of washing up. There was irony in wanting to do something that other people found mundane, but never again being able to. "Maybe boredom is underrated," she pondered, to no one in particular.

Story Book Girl ignored her and searched for a pen amongst the items on the table.

"A clue. I've solved a cryptic clue. 'Journey in the fall,' four letters. The answer is 'trip'."

"Excellent," said Bag Lady, tuning in and clapping her hands unadvisedly – she lost a bit each time. "Then it will all come out in the wash." She shuddered at the thought.

"I'll not shy away from this," proclaimed Bag Lady when Story Book Girl had given up on the crossword and gone upstairs to get dressed. She picked up Ray's wooden hourglass and turned it on its head (the hourglass swore quietly at the imposition; he hated the feeling he got as the sand trickled out of his brain). Story Book Girl had been catapulted into the world and everyone presumed she would come packaged with the wherewithal to cope with human predicaments such as boredom and hopelessness, but Bag Lady had underestimated the extent to which the human creature is shaped by its earthly assignments and Story Book Girl, rightly or wrongly, seemed to consider herself disadvantaged by inexperience. In short, she had no baggage to carry around with her – no carrier bag of mistakes.

"Aha!" Bag Lady pushed the chair back from the table and stood up. She shuffled to the door that led into the forbidden place and struggled to turn the handle with newspaper fingers. "Note to Mouse," she said crossly, "oil the door latch."

With an unusual burst of excitement, she picked up one of her carrier bags and rummaged inside it, muttering.

"So, what have we in here that will make a life for Story Book Girl?" She closed her eyes as if she was playing a party game she remembered, where the point is to feel an item presented by an adult and to guess what it might be. Her newspaper hands, rolled up tightly and tied at the wrist, puckered and gave, and she couldn't feel very much at all. She brought out secateurs, a brush and an old shoe. Then she brought out a small red leather purse with an embossed pattern on the front. It was a purse with many

71

compartments and the pattern was that of a labyrinth. Bag Lady passed the purse from one hand to another, held it to her nose to breath in the strong smell of animal, and lapsed into deep thought.

As morning nodded towards midday, Bag Lady put her arms out in front of her and turned her palms upwards as if appealing for help. She had more up her sleeve than one of Mouse's tissues, and now she was going to use it.

"Journey to an inside place
touched by strife
use chisels to shape a soul
chip away to make the whole
fill a purse with possibility,
fire and spirituality."

Moose returned from his morning walk in the woods and pushed open the front door with his antlers. He wandered absent-mindedly into the kitchen and backed straight out again with wide, scared eyes, when he heard strange noises coming from the room at the back of his house.

The next-door neighbour's chicken laid a fine, speckled brown egg with a spell for a shell, and the next chapter of our story was born.

Chapter Twelve

In which Ray and Story Book Girl cook something up for a special occasion

"So what you are saying," mused Dog, "is that Story Book Girl didn't have a clue that she was part of a bigger story."

"It is very easy for us to think we are travelling on our own, Dog, and for us to fail completely to see the connections between things."

"Like links in a chain then, Eagle?"

"Yes, like links in a chain."

Ray had been in Telford all day, working with the performance group. They found imaginary objects and told stories about their discoveries. The sun shone through the studio windows, and Ray found his thoughts drifting back to the lovely woman he had last seen pegging out the washing at the top of Moose's garden. Hurrying home, he stood at the kitchen door and Story Book Girl acted as if she didn't know he was watching her. She had cleaned the entire house and was sitting at the kitchen table with her legs tucked beneath her, reading Mrs Beeton's Every Day Cookery and Housekeeping Book. A most helpful textbook, advised Bag

Lady, who had found it in a charity shop in Bishop's Castle, on her way to give Nature a progress report.

"Let's cook something for the party!" said Ray, waving his arms in a bizarre manner, to attract Story Book Girl's attention.

Story Book Girl finished reading the paragraph about 'the tired man of business returning home after a harassing day' before she answered.

"But Mouse is doing the cooking."

"Yeah, but we all know that'll be a cheese board and a bowl of cereal," laughed Ray.

Story Book Girl uncurled like a lazy cat and stretched her arms above her head. "I've never cooked."

"All the more reason to try it out; it might be right up your street. It's *nice* to prepare food to share, and cooking is just about imagining how you would like a plate to look and making your wish come true."

"How do we get the food we are going to cook?"

"The garden's a good place to start."

"Won't Mouse be annoyed if we eat his flowers?"

"Not flowers, wally, vegetables. There's enough Moose muck on that vegetable patch to make a country grow."

Ray looked at the door that led into the forbidden place, and on into the back garden. The key was in the keyhole. He had not used the door since the arrival of Bag Lady, feeling instinctively that he would not be made welcome in that part of the house. Thinking better of his intended show of bravado, he took Story Book Girl by the hand (oh, how warm and soft it was) and led her through the hall to the front door (on the latch as usual) and out into the sunshine.

"Find anything?" he asked when they had been on

separate adventures about the garden.

Story Book Girl answered Ray from somewhere inside the greenhouse, behind the washing, at the top of the slopey lawn. "I found some long greens and round reds."

Ray guffawed like a horse. "You mean cucumbers and tomatoes."

"Do I? What funny names. What did you find, clever clogs?"

"Oh, a bit of this and a bit of that," said Ray mysteriously, his hands full of pungent green leaves (sorrel, hawthorn, dandelion, pea shoots) of different shapes and sizes.

They returned to the kitchen with their prizes and decided to check the fridge for interesting items. Predictably, there was cheese – 'Mouserella', Ray called it - and Story Book Girl found a shiny, yellow pepper, some couscous and a squiggel in a cupboard.

"That'll do for starters," declared Ray, rolling up his sleeves. They washed the leaves, span them dry and arranged them in Moose's wooden salad bowl; Ray sliced into the tomatoes, revealing their juicy pulp and yellow-green seeds, and then they added the diced pepper and fresh cut cucumber. Story Book Girl watched as Ray mixed olive oil, sea salt and lemon juice and scattered into it the herbs he had gathered. He poured the dressing over the salad and mixed it in. She chopped the Mouserella cheese (a little guilty at having pilfered Mouse's favourite food after cereal) and sprinkled some of the crumbly white pieces onto the green salad. Some of the mixture flipped out of the bowl and Ray offered it to Story Book Girl, who ate the succulent mouthful from his fingers, finding the crushed herbs, black pepper and garlic with her tongue.

Ray and Story Book Girl were so busy with their creation they didn't hear Mouse come in with extra cheese and cereal for the party guests, and were surprised to see Moose in the kitchen doorway with a bag of shopping on his antlers. Ray looked up and nudged Story Book Girl, who was laughing rather loudly and trying to stuff a whole tomato into her mouth. The seeds ran down her chin and she almost choked when she saw Moose.

Ray patted her on the back and went to help with the bag. "It's party time," he announced happily.

"Happy Birthday," muttered Bag Lady from the rickety 1960's kitchen chair she had installed in the forbidden place. Of course, nobody heard her, as the door from her quarters into the kitchen was always kept closed and locked. She moved her head as quickly as she could to follow the green light that flitted across the frosted window at the back of Moose House, and then turned her head back to look at the locked door as though it might open at any moment.

It was July in Snailbeach and there was to be a party at the village hall that night. Of course, she had been cordially invited, but Bag Lady knew that she made Moose's hair stand on end and Mouse's whiskers twitch, so she had chosen to stay on her own. The party was to welcome the newcomer to the village; the girl they had named Story Book Girl and, as none of them knew when her birthday was, they had unanimously decided that there should be a double celebration.

"How old is she?" Moose had asked Mouse one night, when they had a rare moment to themselves.

"As old as the most lovely woman in the world," Mouse replied after a moment's thought.

"That all depends," considered Moose, "on your point of view. I mean, a younger woman might be energetic and athletic and with not much to say that bears any great wisdom, but might be fine and dandy for a night at the pub with music so loud you couldn't hear her anyway. Whereas an older woman..."

"Oh, do stop waffling, Moose. Perhaps, as Story Book Girl didn't arrive here in any ordinary way, she should be able to pick and choose her years according to her circumstances." Mouse chewed a piece of cheese thoughtfully. "Or perhaps none of us have any choice about the age we really are at any given juncture and life just springs the years upon us randomly, shocking the daylights out of us when we chance to catch a glance in the mirror."

"Now, let's get this straight before we go any further," said Eagle, who was fed up with Dog's tendency to hide under the table when Bag Lady was mentioned.

"Bag Lady was a witch, whiter than white, lighter than light. That does not mean there was not darkness in her heart; the Devil and the dark witches saw to that, but Bag Lady was strong enough to absorb their darkness and direct it inwards, at herself. Of course, that did her no good at all. Like shooting arrows, it pierced her internal organs, attacked her immunity and ate her up a bit at a time. Her skin crinkled and peeled more with every passing day and she walked with a hobble because she wore her toes around her neck on a piece of string. Over the years, Bag Lady learned to mend herself, constructing vital bits and pieces out of organic matter and the paper she found at the side of roads. She carried on putting herself back together and replacing her original body because she thought that once she was gone, the dark witches might join forces and exercise their ferocious power to the full."

Dog nervously scratched his ear with a paw. *"So there are dark witches here in Snailbeach then?"* he asked, feeling the hairs on his back bristle and stand on end.

"Dark witches lurk everywhere," replied Eagle.

Dog disappeared under the table again.

"They hang over power lines, disguised as black plastic bags," she continued, *"or lurk in full view, in schools, shops and hospitals, governments, churches, councils and care homes. They lure creatures in with gifts, promises and contracts and study their weaknesses as if there was a qualification at the end of it. They are strong because they gather the strength of the millions of creatures they have broken, and they delight in the way that those with open hearts and minds follow, admire and*

vote for them. They construct situations particular to the fancy of individuals, which lead them to traps from which there is sometimes no escape."

Dog tried to think of creatures he knew who could be dark witches. He could only think of cauliflower.

"Of course, many creatures find it hard to distinguish between dark witches and white," Eagle continued. "And dark witches are particularly handy with spells which confuse and confuddle. By the time the creature is in the trap that has been prepared for it, it is too distressed to fathom quite how it got there. So we continue to sacrifice our children, have our minds distorted and ruined and we lay a blanket over the light which naturally shines from our souls, so that beams can no longer transmit. Without communication of light, love dies in our community and the Devil and the dark witches have won."

Chapter Thirteen

In which The Villagers are invited to Story Book Girl's party

They began to arrive at half past seven in the evening. The double doors of the village hall were thrown wide open to let the larger creatures through. Mouse hovered by the door, but not too close, as it would be easy for a small furry to get squashed by mortals more muscular. All the neighbours had been invited to Story Book Girl's party and Bag Lady had promised to make sure the bill was paid, although she would not be attending the evening.

"Over here for dwinx," shouted Dolphin, through the hatch at the far end of the hall. She was sitting on the edge of the sink with a wine glass balanced on the end of her nose. Her colleague, Mr Lynx, had forbidden her to serve the food as she always insisted on playing with it so much that paying customers didn't really want to eat it afterwards.

"Over here for Hot Pot," informed Mr Lynx, who may have been a hippo, but in his orange tuxedo, thought he was something else.

The people and other creatures piled into the hall and made themselves comfortable at small tables lit with tea-lights in pretty glass holders of amber and red, purchased from John's Shop. Horse stood on the stage tapping a microphone and messing with his amplifier.

"One, two. One, two," he neighed loudly.

Moose, who once worked as a sound engineer at the BBC, was up there too, adjusting the lights with his antlers, inwardly critical of horse's techniques. By the time everyone had arrived, the hall was warm and shone with pretty twinkles.

Eagle had stayed at Moose House with Story Book Girl, to help her get ready for the occasion. Bag Lady had dipped deep into one of her bags and found a retro dress for her to wear. It was of deep blue satin and once it had been carefully ironed by Eagle (Bag Lady didn't like to get too close to hot things) fitted perfectly in every way. Unlike some Shropshire birds, Eagle hadn't really much patience when it came to preening, but she made the right noises as Story Book Girl adorned herself and paraded through the house, past every available mirror. As Eagle and Story Book Girl walked through the Snailbeach night towards the hall, Story Book Girl looked towards the hills and saw her own moon shadow, huge and faceless upon the dark landscape.

By the time they reached the hall, the party was in full swing. Mr Lynx was pouring endless pints of everything and Dolphin was swishing about in the sink and washing the occasional plate. A table had been set up at the back of the room and people rushed to give Story Book Girl presents wrapped in glitzy paper of every imaginable colour, which she accepted politely and put on the table.

"Why do people give each other pretty boxes?" she asked Mouse; but the music was too loud for him to hear and he just shot her an anxious smile.

Horse sang his two songs with feeling, though Mouse was concerned that they wouldn't get their deposit back if Moose and Horse broke the stage with their hooves.

Then it was Sparrow's turn to sing a song about a starry night – it was amazing how such a small guitar could put out so much sound (Ray told Moose the sound was compressed, but it seemed perfectly happy to Moose).

Magpie climbed onto the stage and sang a beautiful song she had written only that week, to another magpie, of course, who sat and looked up at her in admiration.

"That's my missus," she magged, over and over again.

Later, there was cake – a cheese cake made by Mouse, and a double recipe chocolate one decorated by three young gazelles, who butted each other in their excitement to be first to put it down in front of Story Book Girl. Raven had brought her drums and invited people to play them.

People who did not know they possessed rhythm found something very ancient inside themselves. They worked with their hands, and they worked with their feet. Their fingers grew red and swollen, their shoes pinched tight, but still the rhythm swept them on, building and falling, building and falling, their faces open, eyes wide, souls connected by the beat of hearts and drums.

As the evening yawned and longed for bed, the villagers poured out into the night and dispersed into shadow and quiet, and all but a little gaggle seemed to disappear, returning to everyday lives that hold them to the piece of earth they can most understand.

Of the gaggle, Moose led the way home, singing at the top of his voice, a bag of presents on each antler and an Eagle on his left shoulder. There was a very tall, funky fairy with blonde crinkly hair, who seemed to have forgotten where she lived, but seemed also not to mind as she was still dancing, slightly above the ground.

Mouse was reflecting on the success of the evening and mentally preparing a report for Bag Lady which included the size of the cheque she was going to be asked to write. Story Book Girl and Ray brought up the rear; Ray's arm wrapped around Story Book Girl's waist, so she could feel the warm support of his arm through her thin dress.

Chapter Fourteen

In which Ray and Story Book Girl urm… get to know each other better

When they arrived home after the party, at a place where they were quiet and thought they were quite alone, he called her to him.

"Story Book Girl?"

"Mm?" She jumped when she heard his voice, searching for the meaning of different tones and inflections; wending her way through his consciousness.

"Why don't you come here and relax a while?"

She knew Ray couldn't really understand why she found it difficult to stop. Even when the house was clean and tidy (for some reason, she had taken to vacuuming like a duck to water), when they had cooked the meals and cleared the dishes, Story Book Girl found it difficult to sit still. He sometimes caught sight of her dancing on her own in the fire light, pushing her limbs beyond comfort, seeking to release some uncontrollable energy which she had been given without a guide to its purpose. Anxious to please, and pleased he knew he could anchor her when he wished, she wandered into the living room. They knelt on the threadbare sofa, arms resting across its back, and looked out at the moonlit sky. They still wore their party clothes, and to Badger, who came sniffing in the front garden in his search for juicy snails, they looked like meerkats watching for their mob to return to the burrow.

"A frog," said Ray, pointing at an illuminated cloud, which stretched long, thin, powerful legs and hopped across the sky.

"A bull," insisted Story Book Girl. "And here it comes to get you. Quick, duck!" She grabbed his arm and pulled him down so that, in his laughing surprise, he fell almost on top of her.

She held her hands high, so that she did not need to touch the fine hair that framed his forehead, even though that was what she most wanted to do in the world. The power of eyes…

He reached behind her and traced the shape of her scapula with strong thumbs. Continuing downwards and inwards he focused, puzzled, as he reached an unfamiliar place, and Story Book Girl winced slightly under his touch.

"You have supracoracoideus muscles," he blurted, jumping up to fetch his anatomical colouring book from the shelves where he and Moose had ordered their books alphabetically as a major concession to tidiness.

"I do what?"

"They raise the wings of birds between beats," he continued, returning to the shelf to pick up a book on ornithology, then slowing, stopping, turning to face Story Book Girl, one hand under the book, the back of the other raised to his eye in gesture of a small boy who is suddenly tired.

Story Book Girl stood up and went to him then. She took the book from his hands and put it on the little table; she took both his hands in hers and drew him close to her belly so they breathed in each other's scent.

They had known each other for ever.
They were ancient wild animals of the forest, frolicking and fighting.
They were feathers blowing in a breeze.
They were trees with intertwining branches, shifting through seasons.

She tipped her head back, inviting him to kiss her throat. She groaned beneath the touch of his lips and he groaned too and brushed the hair from her eyes and lifted her face to meet his own.

A fission of colours and minds as their eyes met, bright blue flash shot through with dark slate grey and deep purple indigo. Olive green with rust brown hues and the lightest paintbrush touches of powder blue.

Centuries old defences of men and women, drawing lines in the sand to mark barriers and boundaries, dropped in a second to the synchronised beat of two hearts, together with Nature's magic drum. Firelight threw their swirling shadows onto the walls; beautiful, erotic puppets each finding and losing himself in the other.

Bag Lady opened her eyes and wondered where she was. She had walked in the woods for a while, near to the valve house, a relic from Snailbeach mining days. This was a tiny building of curves and secrets, a covered archway bedecked with earth, oxeye daisies, grasses, ferns and foxgloves, nestled in the woods near to Snailbeach Pool. Under scudding clouds, the rustle of her paper shoes disguised by the warning sound of a watching owl, she had collected medicinal flora. She was pleased with her collection: Chelidonium majus, Mandrake, St John's Wort, cuttings for the garden...

The house was quiet when she returned there, everyone out at the party, and she rested her head on her arms for a moment (just five minutes and I'll be bright as a sparkler). As she let the darkness close in around her, a childhood dream escaped from the depths of her consciousness. Abandoned in a dark, forgotten place lived a half constructed doll. It sat in the centre of an empty room from where it could not move or reach out. Half formed thoughts danced in its head, but it had no mouth and couldn't make a sound.

The Holly King has ears as sharp as prickles. He hears our dreams and eats our happy thoughts when we are most vulnerable in sleep. Lie in the darkness now and hear the knocking of his heart beat.

Knock   Knock   Knock

"Poor Bag Lady," he says, "no-one is ever going to love you. You are old and ugly and your wisdom is wasted on these human creatures. Why, your own daughter is just a story book character who dances with strangers, whilst you sit at home alone. Won't you come and dance with me, Bag Lady?" He turns on his 1960's vintage record player and the needle drops onto the nightmare soundtrack of nothingness.

Chapter Fifteen

In which Story Book Girl and Ray walk in the woods

She wandered here, she wandered there, she wandered
almost everywhere, but what she wondered most of all
was who she was, or not at all.

Who are we? Here are three little words. Here is a pair
of shoes at the door. Here is the silken web of a purple
spider hanging between Story Book Girl and Lost Girl.
Here are secateurs hanging from a rusty hook in the corner
of someone's mind. Here is the shadow of someone's hand
on the wall, reaching out to SNIP......SNIP.....SNIP.

That evening, two lovers walked past the little wooden
gate and under the privet arch at the bottom of Moose
House garden path, avoiding a tiny, unsuspecting black toad
by inches. They turned left, then right, and trudged on up
the hill that tips towards Eastridge woods then rolls and
shifts through the hills. The rough ground, coated with soft,
brown pine needles, muted the sound of footsteps so they
broke the night only with gentle biscuit crunching sounds.
"What's that?"

The two progressed slowly and as their shadowy figures encroached upon the privacy of nocturnal beasties, the black dogs that are everywhere in Snailbeach appeared in front of them and sniffed the air in disdain, disturbed from tasty dreams of bones and rabbits. Ray tore sticks of holly from the bushes that lined the path; their polished leaves reflecting the light of the moon. He threw the sticks towards the animals.

"Sshh," he breathed, putting his finger to his lips.

The animals paused mid-bark, whined moodily and lay down to let Ray and Story Book Girl pass. The weight of the holly sticks crushed the last wild garlic, releasing its scent to create a heady mix with pine, honeysuckle and night-time.

"What's that sound?"

Letting go of his lover's hand, Ray tore off another branch and carried it in front of them like a lance – to ward off mischievous spirits, he told her with a grin. She held his arm and he guided her, whilst she tilted her head skywards to watch skittering bats and twinkling stars.

"The ancient Greeks saw the constellations of the milky way as a smear of milk across the sky and they believed that individual stars were a vast herd of cattle, shepherded by Capella through the rivers of their milk," she told him, and they both wondered how she knew such things when at Moose House it often seemed she knew nothing at all.

The full moon shone bright as Ray and Story Book Girl reached the valve house. The inner gate was padlocked tight against intruders, but they found that Nature had busily prepared a bed of ferns for them inside the entrance.

"What's that sound?"

Kneeling, Ray dug his fingers into the compacted earth outside the shelter and carefully planted his holly branch. "To guard against evil," he said in mock seriousness.

The lovers turned their bodies in towards the other and each swam in the blurred features of their soul mate for the longest of times. They sat in the shelter and drank of the moon and ate of the clouds that played above them. When sleep arrived, they held on to each other as they journeyed far into the night. At that moment, Story Book Girl knew exactly who she was and there was no doubt now about what she desired. She lay willingly upon the warm earth and buried her head beneath her lover's chin.

She had the sense of spines entwined
silver, moonlit, cast out of sleep,
real only until they shift and turn towards morning.

nestled there beneath his chin,
a calm place,
cheek upon the warmth of his chest,
his resting head, her shelter for the night,
his arms her circle of security.

Slipping into sleep,
what beauty to be found in trust so simple.

Chapter Sixteen

In which Story Book Girl encounters the Holly King

"But listen to this," said Eagle to Dog, as they span and bottled honey together (Dog's mouth and paws were very sticky and Eagle noticed he was starting to look pleasantly rounded about his belly). "We cannot undo what is done, so we should think long and hard before we begin. Once a spell is cast we cannot pick and choose the pieces of it we would rather ignore. It may be that now, we would like this to be a simple story, you know, two creatures meet and fall in love and then we leave them to live happily."

Dog stopped with his paw in the air. To some creatures, it seems as if things ought to be straightforward and mainly consist of food, cuddles and rolling over. It was difficult for Dog to imagine complications, although he was learning fast that Eagle's stories were sometimes like an itch without the satisfaction of a good scratch.

"But Moose and Mouse called Bag Lady to Moose House because they thought their friend needed help, and when she was there they could hardly contain their impatience for something more exciting to happen. When Bag Lady and I arrived in Snailbeach we seemed to bring magic with us, and everyone began to think the enigmatic old woman in the forbidden place

had all the answers. Had we all looked around only a little, we might have discovered the long list of mistakes that Bag Lady had made over many years, but we were too busy obsessing about ourselves to be able to see the bigger picture.

Moose, Mouse and Ray moaned and complained and Bag Lady perceived a way of pleasing them all, whilst cleverly complying with Nature's wishes."

"And that was when Story Book came along," Dog joined in, making sure he'd got the plot.

"Yes, and time went by and we all began to settle down and be more or less content with what we had together. But by this time, Bag Lady had hatched a plan that she thought would keep Nature happy, whilst seeming to please us all. We may have broken some rules by inviting magic into the house; we were also fickle, because when things began to go well on their own, we put aside any guilt or misgivings and merrily got on with our new lives. We clean forgot about the strange old lady living in the back room and didn't ever really understand her connection with Story Book Girl.

"Craaaaackle," grinned the egg as it knew what its purpose in life was to be. EGG SPELL is the first line of defence against the entry of bacteria; it can be brown or white.

"Whoooooosh," fancied the egg as it rolled out the neighbour's chicken coop, pithered about in the garden, bounced through the farmyard and up the hill into the woods. As it rolled, it gathered speed and substance until it was like a round snowball cloud trapped in the Shropshire Hills.

93

"Buuuuuzzzzzz," heckled the egg as it heard voices in the valve house. There are approximately eight to ten thousand tiny pores which allow moisture and gases in and out of an egg.

"What's that sound?"

"Meeeee," clucked the egg as it stretched, split, crouched and waited to pounce. There are two membranes on the inside of the shell. One membrane sticks to the shell and one surrounds the white. These are the second line of defence against bacteria. They are composed of thin layers of protein fibres.

Ray and Story Book Girl slept in the woods.
The spell pounced.

Story Book Girl groaned in her sleep. Shrouded figures shifted inside the valve house as her dreams took on the forms usually reserved for reality. She strained to see in the gloom and failing this she was confused, thinking she may be blind.

She crawled out of the valve house, and on sleeping legs she rose to dance with the Holly King, who held her tight with hands of darkness pressed at her back, and kissed her against her will. As he pivoted around her, unforgiving, honed muscles enjoying the close proximity of her small, soft body, her abused spirit shook itself free, threw itself down and dug its nails deep into the undergrowth. The fingers and toes of the trees that clutch the earth discovered it there, hot and crumpled, and dug a hole to hide it and keep it from dying.

When the music ended and the Holly King released her, the inside of her head felt as if it had been filled with marbles, and cold shadows clutched at her eyes. She stumbled past the holly branch and the cocoon where her dream spirit lay buried, and walked into the night – lost.

I wonder if we are ever or never alone.
I wonder if we are meant or not to fall.
Perhaps there is a safety net,
protective arms which spread
to catch us, hup, and laugh.
Yet
Perhaps we are only one,
below us just a void,
made nothing by fear and compromise,
as wide as our eyes in the dark,
as deep as the loss of our dearest friend.

A small fire had been lit behind the valve house and the orange light and smell of burning holly was comforting. Story Book Girl held out her hands to receive the warmth. Crouching by the fire she picked up a knife and a walking stick. The knife handle had been licked by the fire, and Story Book Girl flinched as it blistered her palm, but she held onto it, instinctively feeling it might afford her some kind of protection. She turned her back on the shelter where her lover lay sleeping and felt the earth incline as she climbed a track deep into the woods. Somewhere in front of her a robin sang in the night and she felt compelled to follow its sound with her feet.

Gradually, as her delicate skin became accustomed to the bristling undergrowth and the sky lost the light of the moon and turned an eerie green, she began to take notice of her surroundings. She was in a rolling place where the hills met the sky, and the fir trees that framed the edges of the rounded hills became bent and weathered guardians of the landscape. They watched Story Book Girl climb away from her life in Snailbeach village and travel where the moon no longer threw its shadow. She wandered into the Picture of the Green Green Woods and further and further from what she knew.

Chapter Seventeen

In which Mouse has a dream and Ray comes home alone

Moose was dreaming. In his dream he was running across a frozen field with Derw, son of Moose. Moose's dream took them to Nipstone Rock, where craggy hills were exposed to wind, which teased them with blustering blasts, wrapping the ice tightly around the two happy, healthy beasts.

Derw's antlers hung with icicles, which jangled as he gambolled ahead of his father, smiling with the joy of freedom and companionship. Occasionally Moose tripped and laughed out loud, enjoying the challenge of running wild and rough with the younger stag.

Moose was cold. He turned over in bed and drew the covers up to his furry chin.

Eagle listened to the big animal making moose noises. His breathing was heavy and punctuated with gaps where the dream wind caught his breath and dragged it away from him. Eagle turned her attention to Moose's beautiful face. On his large brow was etched a map which alternated between an expanse of clear pastureland with true and sure footed pathways, and unsteady, furrowed land, difficult to navigate. Eagle sighed and turned away, tucking her beak into her feathered breast in an attempt to rest.

It wasn't yet light. Each day when virgin light came to Snailbeach, it was defiled by the spiked fingers of a Montgomery oak tree outside Ray's window. Because of this it was reticent and waited to be called by the farm cockerel. Mouse knew that it was not much past four in the morning when he stirred, the cockerel still sleeping, the dawn still cowering. Mouse's whiskers twitched as they explored familiar places. He would drift off for ten minutes, he decided, rubbing his nose with sleepy paws.

But something had rattled him and curiosity rose in his belly like a poppy seed. Anxiety fluttered, forcing his little head to rise and his fuddled morning brain to tick. What had disturbed him in the middle of the night? A draught through the letter box? A noise in the garden shed? Mouse scrambled to his feet, sniffing the air. He scanned the room: bed, chair, socks, boxes, story books, all as they had been.

The noise had been a door, a downstairs door. The doors upstairs dragged on carpet and would not have clicked so decisively. Had anyone arrived, welcome visitor or intruder, Ray would have met them at the door - relief briefly replaced concern...

But lately Ray had been exhausted in the mornings, hardly able to crawl out of bed. He complained of fever and was sometimes flushed. Mouse had been worried, but when he mentioned it at breakfast yesterday, Moose had turned away, his broad shoulders shaking, and even Eagle, who seldom laughed out loud, had curled up her wing feathers and mumbled something in mock annoyance about the delirium of love getting in the way of a good night's sleep.

Mouse was suddenly filled with botheration. The only thing to do was to wake Eagle and Moose. He couldn't understand why the whole household wasn't trying to clear up the mystery; but to somebody as small as Mouse a hardly audible click is magnified one thousand fold in importance.

Mouse knocked on the bedroom door, then knocked louder to be heard over the snoring of an eight hundred pound slumbering Moose. Eagle sprang awake and pretended she had never slept (it was some source of pride to Eagle that she had eyes four times as sharp as Ray's with much less dozing).

"I think the world might have ended," exclaimed Mouse, scampering into the bedroom without waiting to be invited. The tiniest teardrop made its way down one of his whiskers.

"Huh?" said Moose, rubbing his nose with a stray hoof.

"Something has changed in Moose House, and I don't know what to think it is," Mouse continued, waving his paws theatrically. Eagle stared, open beaked, at her small friend.

"Mouse, this is a bit early for you to be so lively; maybe you should take more lettuce with your cheese?"

"I heard a click, and then…"

"Then?" Moose and Eagle held their breath involuntarily; the way parents might when they sense their child is about to offer some profound insight.

"Then, nothing," continued Mouse, but he was already pulling Moose (ineffectually, it has to be said) towards the bedroom door.

Ray wasn't clear what time it was when he woke and found her gone. The ferns where she had lain were still etched with the shape of her body; his hand was still warm where he had curled it around hers when they had finally slept. But the space beside him was dark and empty and his heart was immediately filled with foreboding. Ray closed his eyes tightly in an attempt to stop giddiness preventing him from taking action. His gentle eyelids pressed tears from his eyes and he stumbled blindly from the shelter.

It was daybreak when he reached the house and he was just in time to meet Moose, Eagle and Mouse closing the door behind them as they left for the hills. Moose stopped in the lane as he saw Ray swaying towards him. He knew this man like his own tail: when he was well he was tall and strong, his presence hypnotic; even at a distance Moose knew Ray was sick at heart. Mouse, who sees hidden things as well as Eagle sees faraway places, knew he had been right to be worried all along.

Ray spoke slowly, as if in a dream: "I think Story Book Girl has been stolen."

Mouse gasped, Moose stumbled and Ray's legs buckled. Eagle was there at his shoulder, great wings holding him up, propelling him firmly towards the house.

"Where's Bag Lady?" she asked her companions, her voice full of concern and impatience. Bag Lady knew so much that she never spoke about, but not speaking sometimes made her invisible and Ray needed real support.

"In the forbidden place," quaked Mouse. "She came back when we were getting ready, and shut herself in there, muttering and fumbling."

Eagle lifted Ray into the house and he went straight to kneel upon the sofa, his eyes upon the clouds. Some kind of uneasy peace rested upon him then and Eagle went to tap on the locked wooden door that led to 'the forbidden place'.

After what seemed an eternity, Bag Lady put the door knob back on its spindle and opened the door a crack. Eagle looked beneath the bristling eyebrows into the faded, inscrutable ricepaper eyes, and the two creatures communicated without words, as if genetically bound.

Bag Lady nodded and waited for Eagle to back off and turn around before closing and locking the door behind her and putting the key into the large single pocket on the front of her tunic. She shuffled without hurry into the living room. Ray didn't look up; sat on the sofa, feet crossed and legs curled under him, a tragic pantomime aimed at no-one in particular. Bag Lady stood, hands on hips, in front of his glazed eyes, her breath rasping as she considered his state of mind. She nodded again in Eagle's direction and Eagle reluctantly left the house. Meanwhile, Bag Lady took a small phial from her pocket and administered a green-black potion to the unseeing Ray.

Chapter Eighteen

In which Bag Lady's plan is revealed – well, a bit anyway

Bag Lady had planned Story Book Girl's journey carefully. During interminably long team meetings with Nature and Nature's other long serving employee, Time, they discussed a long term mission, which was to harness Good, using the skills and attributes that humans have to offer, in order to overcome Evil and give hope to the world. But the notion of an army of any sort is abhorrent to Nature, as armies have been used by Evil for so long, it is hard to imagine that anything positive could be achieved by one.

The alternative was to bring about change by altering the stories of chosen individuals. As a lover of stories, Bag Lady seemed, to Nature, to be the ideal team leader for this project. But it was becoming clear that an epic like this would not be easy to orchestrate.

From her own experiences stretching back over lonely decades, Bag Lady had developed the notion that there exist truths which, collectively, could equip a being to live for one perfect moment – that is, one moment as a person who is polished so pure that we could see through them. Like a piece of bread sliced so thin that it becomes something holier than bread, or a cobweb so fine it hardly exists, yet is strong enough to hold a string of dew drops without breaking. Bag Lady didn't claim to know all the truths herself, but believed the time had come to put her idea into practise – at the same time turning her flawed creation experiment into a triumph for the cause of Good.

Bag Lady had wandered through the ancient Snailbeach landscape and upon the Stiperstones hills, and picked out secrets accessible only to the initiated. She bought an ordnance survey map at John's shop in Stiperstones, spread it out and stared at it for hours. The woods and contoured hills etched themselves onto her memory – the shape of the woods resembling an old witch bending to eat Snailbeach. She rifled through Mouse's belongings and found some post-it notes, on which she wrote numbers and symbols and the names of places, so she knew the route that would be travelled and approximately the time it would take. Bag Lady chuckled with rare pleasure as she became therapist, chemist, geographer, diviner and manager. She extracted and blended flower and animal essences, read books that no-one else could make any sense of, and went over and over the plans in her mind until her nose began to bleed.

Bag Lady's plan was not completely altruistic – very few plans are. She had waged war with dark witches, unhappy circumstances and unfortunate happenings all her life and frankly, was physically worn out by her work, which seldom went smoothly. Enter Story Book Girl, a young, healthy woman invested of her own endeavour, bursting with wasted energy, inspired by the imagination of a highly creative individual and created by Nature herself. By the time Story Book Girl returned to Snailbeach following a short sojourn in the Green Green Woods, she would surely possess the wherewithal to defeat the darkness, according to Nature's project – leaving Bag Lady free to skip the light fantastic, over the hills and far away.

Of course, like so many middle managers, she declined to discuss the details of her plan with the creatures involved. She knew how easy it was for good ideas to be blocked and progress halted by sceptics like Mouse. So it was that on the night of the party, when Moose, Mouse, Ray and Story Book Girl had left for the village hall, Bag Lady took a bottle of warm auburn hair dye, mixed it with holly solution and essence of wolf and shook the concoction until it thickened and changed colour, from green, through rose to indigo. Pleased so far, she made herself at home upon the moose sofa and breathed an incantation entirely comprised of the items she could see on the mantelpiece and hanging around the fire. These were the gifts she would give to Story Book Girl.

The Statue of a Lost Girl, a Wooden Painted Wolf, a Photograph of a Woman with a Big Smile, a Calculator, a Painting of a Road, an Empty Tin, a Feather, Sheep Wool, a Book, a Salt Lamp, a Glass of Water, a Picture of a Green Green Wood, a Blue Matchbox Lorry, a Boat, a Banana, Eight Little Figures Hanging from a Wooden Hoop, a Shell Full of Money, a Guitar, a Ball of Finger Knitting, Something Folded she thought was the Map Of The Hills she had prepared earlier - but wasn't.

That should be enough to start her off, Bag Lady told herself, in the belief that things are chosen by the eye for a reason. Anyway, it was all a bit of an experiment, wasn't it? Nothing to lose...

Book Two

Chasing their Tales

Eagle slapped the warm, dead chicken onto the kitchen table and coughed to remove the feathers lodged at the side of her beak. She would process it later, when the neighbours had quietened down outside – humans round here seemed to think they were the only ones entitled to catch and eat chicken. She guessed Dog was asleep upstairs. She had tried to ignore the effect that hearing the stories had on him, anxious to have them written before anything could get in the way, but Dog began to act very strangely and had been visibly upset at the untimely disappearance of Story Book Girl, which left Moose, Mouse and Ray in a world never to be the same again.

"Why did she go?" he asked, over and over again. "Why didn't she stay with Ray?" Dog had spent time in a kennel for homeless dogs, through no fault of his own, but was a loyal character. He began to pine for his new master and this was compounded by the stories Eagle had told about home and belonging. She knew she would have to let him go soon, but had grown fond of her friend and his quirky interpretation of her tales.

Eagle hopped up the twiggy stairs and put her head round the bedroom door.

"Dog?"

But Dog was nowhere to be seen.

Chapter One

In which Nature is late for work and Time takes off

"Fandango!" spat Nature under her breath as the front wheel of her bicycle scraped against the kerb and she was unceremoniously tipped onto the road, engendering the wrath of parents ferrying reluctant children to school.

"Fandango Biluchi!"

She picked herself up, more embarrassed than hurt, and struggled to get her bike out of the path of oncoming traffic. Unable to smile, she shrugged in what she hoped was an apologetic manner and proceeded to guide the bike along the pavement with her feet firmly on terra firma.

She hadn't been concentrating. There was a letter on headed paper in her rucksack from none other than his bliddy Majesty the Holly King.

"*Dear Cousin,*" he inscribed in neat scratchy handwriting. Being of a certain age, he always handwrote his own letters and this being the case they had the immediate impact of a knife being forced up between one's ribs.

"*I am concerned to hear that your prodigy, Story Book Girl, appears to have absconded. Please accept my condolences.*

On a more optimistic note, I am delighted to announce the impending romantic engagement between the talented Ms Bag Lady and myself. I have long felt that we were meant for each other. My intended and I will be holding a modest 'shindig' to mark the occasion (further details to follow) to which, of course, you are cordially invited.

Yours sincerely Mr H King

"You have got to be having a laff!" Nature held the letter up to the light to check for evidence of fraud, but yes, there was the holly leaf watermark that lay behind every disastrous communication she had ever had with the King of Darkness. So Bag Lady had finally switched allegiances had she? Well fiddle dee dee. Just what damage had been done by a keeper of stories acting so irresponsibly, Nature found it difficult to gauge. If stories of hope were spun to become stories of darkness it could signal the end of everything. Nature had pulled on a polyester cardigan that stretched tight across her substantial bosom, shoved the letter in her rucksack and hurried out of the back door, beckoning her bike on the way through the yard. Like the rest of Telford, she had to get to the office, tout suite!

"May I ask where you are going?"

It was nearly lunchtime in Telford, and the team meeting called by Nature that morning had only just ended. Time, who had tried to be quiet on his way through Nature's office to the car park, stopped in his tracks and shrugged; it was no good attempting to get one past Nature, the wily old bat.

"Pardon?" he mumbled.

"I said, where are you going?" Nature peered at him over the top of her reading glasses.

"Look, boss, I'm not needed in this bit, right? I mean Story Book Girl is in the Picture of the Green Green Woods, where Time is redundant, outmoded, laid off, right?"

Nature's thumb pressed the clicky thing on her pen – click, click, click. She had already broken one pen that morning. "It would be short-sighted of me to let you go at this point, Time," she said. "Story Book Girl might be lost in the woods where time is – er–not of the essence, but there are a whole lot of other creatures who appreciate having you around to impose order on their lives. They know the small hand of the clock makes two revolutions every one of their days, whilst the big hand confidently circles twenty four times and then begins again, over and over until they step off the planet, and they are reassured that after they die the hands will continue to circle in exactly the same way to accommodate the lives of their children and their children's children." Nature doodled concentric circles in the margin of her notebook and didn't check whether Time was listening or not before she continued.

"On this presumption, they organise their daily affairs, allotting a predictable amount of Time to such as cleaning their teeth and travelling to work." She sliced the circles with her pen. "Even though Bag Lady, before totally losing the plot, exceeded her remit by casting an open ended spell which simultaneously lost the main character of our story and threw the others into chaos, I'm sure when we get to the other end of this predicament, it will be good to have you around."

Time sighed; to be honest he was bored by Nature's ramblings. His work was relentless and complicated these days, as humans took affairs into their own hands and ignored the helpful systems he had designed to make things unambiguous. He revelled in bringing about change in the lives of creatures tied to him by an invisible thread, but longed to experience first hand the thrill of life 'happening' to him as it happened to them: the freefall of experience.

Reading the thoughts of her longest serving employee and aware that he had fallen out of love with his work, Nature had a spark of inspiration, more unusual since she had been prescribed Benzodiazepine medication in the wake of the Suez crisis of 1956.

"You could always go and look for her," she suggested, totting up the benefits of having Time away whilst she sorted out the general scheme of things and the mess that Bag Lady had got them all into. Somehow, the world had become muddled; perhaps if she put aside Time, she would be able to work on one problem without causing another.

"Look for whom?" asked Time, giving himself the opportunity to consider Nature's offer; he hadn't had a day off for almost fourteen billion years and was owed paid holiday. He estimated it would take him five minutes, forty three seconds and six attoseconds to pack an overnight bag and wing it out of the backside of Telford before lunchtime rush hour. Nature, who complained of being short of cash as a result of the current political and economic climate, was in the habit of renting offices in most undesirable locations.

"Story Book Girl, of course. And if you happen to come across Bag Lady – give her a piece of my mind!"

Time considered that Nature might not have much to spare. "Thanks, boss," he said out loud, "it's a deal."

Pushing her glasses back to the bridge of her nose, Nature looked down at her work. "Don't forget to leave your holiday form on the way out," she reminded him.

But Time had already left the building.

Chapter Two

The Holly King's story

High up on the hills above Snailbeach, is a smattering of ruined homesteads that for generations were shelter to miners and their families. Most are uninhabitable, but one or two have withstood the ravages of Snailbeach winters and in one of these - lived a king.

The Holly King was a farmer of sorts, with his roots firmly established in the Stiperstones hills. For many years he fed his cattle and looked out at Hope valley, knowing it would never change. In June each year, he would take delivery of logs from his twin, the Oak King, and begin to prepare for the onset of winter. At the winter solstice, when the Earth's axial tilt is farthest away from the sun, he would put on a thick sheepskin coat and venture out to touch each holly tree with his hands. The trees bowed down to him and the land slept.

Things could have remained the same for ever, but seldom do. Whilst people worked upon the land, the seasons held their time and attention. But towns grew into cities wilder than the woods, and as people moved further and further from the influence of the hill, they forgot what it was to be still.

Lives became tangled and frenetic; folks shopped, partied and demanded more and more from the earth. The Holly King was outraged – in the general scheme of things, he hadn't asked for much.

"Be off with you!" he snapped at the very creatures who had chosen to stay behind. "Go and live in expensive new houses, spend your money and see if it brings you happiness. He sent them scurrying, and even banished his own son, Time, a bit of a hippy who argued that the whole affair was just 'a sign of the times'.

Actions have consequences: without Time, things on the hill stagnated; without people, houses fell down; and without cattle, the holly trees lost their sense of purpose and began to die. In the year 1986, during the month of April, the Holly King's anger was replaced by malice so cold that hailstones weighing one kilogram each, fell in Bangladesh.

"*My Dear Nature,*" he wrote, "*I have decided to organise a festival.*"

"A festival?" Nature had been appalled, beset by images of tons of litter and overflowing toilets.

She wrote back: "Over my dead body!"

The King was not put off. Masquerading as a farmer seeking to diversify, he visited a bank in Shrewsbury, signing himself Mr H King. Making full use of 'rural regeneration', 'value added' and 'enterprise' buzzwords in his business pitch to the manager, he wangled himself a hefty loan. Without further ado, he acquired marquees and equipment, put an advert in the Shropshire Star for staff and contacted Snailbeach's resident journalist to publicise the event:

PRESS RELEASE

The Pink Cake Fest (sponsored by creative cakes limited)

is where problems lie low when they can not be sorted and no-one must know.

When you ought to say something but maybe you won't and the words to explain are all wrong, so you don't.

Where dreams interrupted meet goals never scored or your clothes are too small and you can't afford more.

When there isn't an answer or nothing quite makes it or something is missing or somehow you break it.

When you thought that you had it and then you forgot

Come on up, eat pink cake and rescue the plot!

For further information contact

Hking@betree.com

After an initial slow response, social networks twigged, visitors arrived, and as Nature lost control, the festival expanded. The Holly King's plan to win people back was a success, but the festival never claimed to be a social enterprise and, in the nature of many capitalist ventures, it grew from greed, rather than need.

As Time no longer lived on the hill, the festival had no end, which was great for business. Profit margins increased as Mr King underwent a steep learning curve in his new business realm and made the most of escalating unemployment to spin the idea of free labour into something desirable. But whilst festivals can be fun places to be on a sunny weekend, by Sunday night people are generally ready to pack up and go home. The Holly King found himself surrounded by several thousand bored, tired and not very clean members of the General Public, made grumpy by the overconsumption of junk food. He did two things: employed people to keep order, and invented a game.

He had come to realise that the festival goers attracted to this out of the way venue were usually lost – figuratively, if not physically. Many had abandoned their own stories and were searching for alternatives. Fabulous! Mr King bought a job lot of 'possibilities, conundrums and universal truths' from a well-known supermarket and after problems with the satellite navigational system, which insisted the route to the hill was via the impassable Bogey Lane, they arrived in a van stacked with hundreds of cardboard boxes. With the help of his employees, he hid his purchases in a zillion places around the festival field.

Rules of the game

1. Each player chooses a bag.

2. As they move around the ~~bored board~~ festival, travelling from left to right, they discover possibilities and solve problems, collecting mistakes and corresponding solutions in their own particular bag.

3. The game ends when there are more problems left than solutions. The game has some intricacies – so that a solution to one player's problem may create problems for other players, which in turn will need solutions.

Indeed, after a relatively short time, the king's employees noted a disproportionate number of problems loitering with intent.

Chapter Three

In which Story Book Girl becomes Lost Girl and stories collide

Stories have their own boundaries and horizons, and the characters within them generally stay there, for better or for worse. In certain circumstances, however, stories collide, and worlds perfectly formed in their own right merge to become sticky and unappetizing. Characters getting on perfectly well inside their own story may suddenly encounter experiences for which they are quite unprepared. It isn't just a matter of meeting and moving on; they are each caught up in the other's consciousness and damaged in the process.

Story Book Girl wandered in the Picture of the Green Green Woods and perversely, the only thing she could think of was the life in Snailbeach she had once wanted to leave. Sinking her bare feet in a rotting leaf mound, she arched her back to watch the oak trees debate with the pea-soup sky. The air in the woods is as clammy as a warm, wet sponge – it hasn't come from anywhere and has nowhere else to go, so it is rather disinclined to exert itself.

"You'll be on your way to the Pink Cake Festival." The voice echoed as if it had travelled through a long pipe and Story Book Girl inhaled sharply at the unexpected sound. A disconnected mouth fell to the ground in front of her; three legs, a pelt and an ancient skull dangled from branches like talismans. Story Book Girl knew nothing of fear or fairy tales: she collected the pieces and fixed the broken creature together as well as she could, admiring her work whilst it coughed and gasped.

The crooked wolf looked at the girl and saw tender, young meat – he hadn't eaten for over four hundred years, and his last meal had ended badly. Pulling himself together, he approached Story Book Girl on the tips of his three paws, his breath warm and damp.

"Festival?"

"They tell me it's one *wild* gig."

The howl of the hungry wolf echoed through the ages and Snailbeachers shivered in their beds.

"We have to hurry if you are going to get a ticket; if the Nosy Parkers arrive at the gate and see you trying to get in, you probably never will."

"Nosy Parkers?"

"Red faced creatures employed by Mr King. They are made entirely of rules and regulations; all white noise and airbrush. Ears filled with white noise can't hear the music. Listen..."

Story Book Girl heard the freesh freesh freesh of a crow's wing beat, the crunch of a slug's twenty seven thousand teeth chewing upon a dead leaf.

"Well, if the Nosy Parkers don't want people to enjoy the festival, why does it still happen?"

"If you have to search too long for a reason, there probably isn't a good one. Come along now."

The wolf bent his neck so she could climb on his back. When she tentatively tapped his rump with the end of her holly stick, the way she had seen Ray playing 'horse' with Moose, he curled his lip, but unimpressed by Story Book Girl's slight weight, resolved to change his story. He limpety limped on the pads of his feet - tramp, squelch, shluk, across the Picture of the Green Green Woods, through ankle deep mud and rusty puddles.

They travelled across and around the woods and Story Book Girl suspected they had taken a wrong turn. The wolf seemed unconcerned and in the absence of the chronology normally imposed by Time, it wasn't clear whether they were coming or going.

At the first corner of the third path, a man stood by a gate hung with a pink painted sign:

WELCOME TO THE PINK CAKE FESTIVAL
'PROUDLY SPONSORED BY CREATIVE CAKES LIMITED'

The man moved his lips, rocked and shook a tin up and down, up and down, silent as an empty promise.

Story Book Girl looked away, but out of the corner of her eye she contemplated the neat figure dressed in an expensive suit and shiny shoes.

"Got a festival ticket and a wrist band for the girl?" said the wolf.

The man searched Story Book Girl's face while she and the wolf waited, but he was in no hurry to give them a ticket.

"I am The Truth, of course," he announced eventually in a tinkling tone, by way of introduction, though no one had asked.

"The Truth?" The wolf tossed his head and winced as the movement dislodged his broken neck. "I heard there is someone goes by the name of Nietzsche at the festival that could help you get your thing together."

"Thank you," said the man, "I will certainly look out for him. Now, that will be sixty minutes for an adult ticket, no concessions." He reached into his briefcase and brought out a form. Pointing at its various boxes, he said, "You will need to sign here, here, and here - oh, and here."

"Sixty *minutes?* Um... please could you give us tickets now if we promise to pay later?"

The man scowled. "Yes, yes, that is what they all say – we'll pay you when we find the Time, but they never do because he doesn't live here any more. It is hardly surprising I got cynical. Time is what we need here - time to think, time to sort things out, time to live a little. I need time to help people find me." He rattled his empty tin.

"Can't you just stand somewhere a bit more obvious?"

The man held Story Book Girl's arm firmly as he fastened her festival wristband - tight. "Little miss know all," he muttered. "You would think you might know The Truth if it looked you in the eye."

Story Book Girl pulled away, walked to the gate and felt along its length for a latch, then realised that the wolf had no intention of accompanying her.

"No, no, no, Story Book Girl, the Pink Cake Festival is a human affair. You won't find many four legged creatures – or three legged ones, for that matter - on that side of the gate." He tossed his head painfully towards another painted sign:

"ABSOLUTELY NO WOLVES."

"Don't worry, Story Book Girl, there is plenty of company at the Festival. Everyone is trying to find a new story since Nature lost the plot. Laughing, he turned and limped back into the woods.

"Coming?" asked the man who called himself The Truth, holding open the gate.

Story Book Girl looked back through the gloom, but didn't recognise anything. Forward seemed the most hopeful direction, but the open gate seemed so heaped with anticipation that to enter was to risk disappointment. There was also the matter of being lost. When someone at Moose House lost something, housemates either helped look for it, or did their best to ignore the search. But *being* the something that is lost seemed more complicated. What happens to the something's identity? How is the something meant to behave?

The feelings of consternation brought about by possibility were unhelpful and the man who called himself Truth had a way of staring, which made her look down at her clothes. She picked at her wristband. ADMIT ONE LOST GIRL, she read.

"Lost Girl. That must be me, then." She congratulated herself for making such an informed deduction, and followed the man who called himself The Truth through the gate.

The Pink Cake Festival was in full swing. Three large marquees topped with pink flags, the seductive smell of spicy burgers, sizzling sausages, candyfloss, cakes and something fishy, wafting from smaller bell tents. The clearing in the

Green Green Woods buzzed with the chatter of hundreds of human beings, mostly with their mouths full. Just about everyone carried a bag of some description, some full to bursting point, others new and empty. The field was so big that by the time the odd couple reached the centre of activities, following the signs from left to right, their feet ached. The man who called himself The Truth stopped to talk to a Nosy Parker in a luminous pink overcoat. He pointed back towards the gate and the Nosy Parker looked agitated.

"Just making sure there is someone on gate duty," explained the man who called himself The Truth, as he caught up with Lost Girl. "You see, the festival is constantly being reorganised. New arrivals come here because they believe it is a good place to be, but struggle with the idea of leaving well alone. Nobody is sure why they are here and there are so many rules that people are usually too anxious to enjoy themselves."

Lost Girl yawned and peered into the marquee, empty except for plumes of steam rising from a kettle at the centre. Her eyes followed the steam upwards to the shape of an artist surrounded by mushrooms. Excited, she span around to tell the man who called himself The Truth what she had found, but he was already mincing towards the smell of roasting pork. Lost Girl saw that she had been mistaken and the mushrooms were steam sheep chomping nonchalantly through meadows of green sky, marking time with docked triangular tails.

The artist was building a sculpture out of books, pressing the wisdom of preserved stories into something new. His chin was set in concentration and the sculpture smelled of old paper, dust and something else. He wrapped each book in plaster-soaked bandages and laid one on top of another, like oatcakes. Each time he had bound two books he picked up a blob of sheep dung, squeezed it until it was sticky, and used it to glue the sculpture together.

"Is this art? I thought animals were barred."

The artist was engrossed in his artistic process and seemed not to hear.

"Here we go again. Don't tell me you're The Truth too?" laughed Lost Girl.

He wiped a strand of hair away from those vaporous eyes, leaving white plaster marks on his forehead. His lined face was interesting and no longer young.

"The art is to step out of our everyday lives in order to see things anew; to shift the universe a fraction."

"But no-one seems to be taking any notice.

"Hold a mirror up to your soul and you will find all the attention you need."

"What will you do with...?"

"Nothing. Soon it will be time to make different shapes in another place. This is intended to be an interactive piece, maybe you could help me."

Lost Girl laughed. "I'm not an artist."

The artist shrugged, leaned down and handed Lost Girl a bandaged book. "Have it if you like, I'm going to take a break now; a Nosy Parker spotted my sheep and is trying to get me evicted." He took the kettle off the boil, releasing the sheep into the atmosphere, and followed Lost Girl out of the marquee, carrying a large, black portfolio; his watery outline faint against the light. His eyes never fixed upon one thing and he flitted between trees, deftly snipping faces out of leaves and hanging them on nodules to be discovered. They followed a path that spiralled down towards a stream marking the outer edge of the festival field. Close to the stream stood a small tent full of people seated on the ground, legs folded and eyes closed.

Lost Girl stood on tiptoe to look over the artist's shoulder. "What are they doing?"

"Shhhh. Meditating. Everyone here is absorbed in solving impossible problems and fully exploring opportunities without the inconvenience of running out of Time. That is why they come. If Time returned, everything might try to catch up with itself and happen in the same moment, with disastrous consequences."

A teenage girl dressed in a graduate's cap, gown and festival wellies, with a school bag over her shoulder, skittered by on a parallel path.

"There's someone I'd like to smother," she called out.

"What?"

"I said has anyone seen my mother?"

The artist made a boat of twigs, with a leaf for a sail, and set it on the water. "She might be in our boat." It caught in an eddy, then careered down the stream.

"Where is it going?" asked Lost Girl, fascinated by the speed at which the boat sailed out of sight.

"To the sea," replied the artist, his demeanour growing fainter as his watery constitution was drawn towards its source.

"Is the sea very far?" Her spirits rose; she had heard Moose talk of Western-Super-Mare with its sea spray and sandy beaches, and felt sure that if she could ever find it, the power of the sea would help her find the way home.

Before the artist could answer, the teenager slid down the hill towards them, to sit on an upturned log by the river.

"What do you want of a mother?" asked Lost Girl.

"Everyone is looking for their mother," the teenager replied. "I learned that earlier today." She reached inside her school bag and brought out a certificate.

"That absolutely isn't the Truth. I haven't even got a mother."

"Then you'll be trying to find the one inside yourself."

Lost Girl wondered if Bag Lady had a mother inside her and imagined she would be pretty screwed up.

"What will you talk about with your mother, if you find her?"

"Oh, nothing much," said the teenager with a shrug. "We rarely see eye to eye."

"So the point is...?"

"The point?" repeated the teenager, rolling the word around her tongue. She stood up and, pulling Lost Girl to her feet, faced up river. "Precisely. By the time we arrive at 'the point', things back at the start are probably not the same. We unwittingly carry the past into the future without knowing the present at all."

Needing help to understand the logic of someone untouched by life's contradictions, Lost Girl looked around for the artist, who seemed to have evaporated. Further along the river bank, a Purple Elf was arguing with a Nosy Parker who was insisting she would have to leave the festival unless she got rid of her dog.

"Who are you?" asked Lost Girl, thinking the elf particularly courageous for bringing her dog to the festival. Lost Girl bent down to stroke the animal, who looked strangely familiar and wagged his tail so hard his body swayed from side to side.

"Who are you?" reflected the Purple Elf, looking her up and down.

Unsure of the answer, Lost Girl left the teenager to philosophise and followed the river's path as it turned a corner and twisted out of sight. Sunlit leaves formed a tunnel of warmest yellow and softest green, which smelled of springtime, and a guild of story weavers nodded to her from where they worked at their looms.

A Scientist who had come to the Green Green Woods to collect three hundred thousand types of beetle without missing her project deadline, scattered a handful of scientific problems on the ground, and the people following her raced to add them to their collection. Lost Girl looked flummoxed by a theory of consciousness she discovered under a tree.

"I would like to give you a present," said the Scientist when the General Public had gathered up her problems and solutions and continued on their way. She reached into the woven orange carpetbag, the tangle of happy mistakes hanging from her shoulder, and took out a creased and folded document.

"Is it a map?" asked Lost Girl hopefully.

"Not a map," replied the scientist. "A periodic table."

"There *is* no map then."

"It is a key," the scientist explained. She sighed, no one

knew about alchemy anymore. "When you reach a door, think carefully before you open it." Smiling, she folded herself up and climbed into the carpetbag.

Lost Girl stood and gaped, then picked up the bag, put the periodic table, book, stick and knife inside it, and walked back to the festival field.

Overwhelmed by wisdom, and on the off chance she might find the artist, Lost Girl headed towards the smell of pork, distracted briefly by an argument between the man who called himself The Truth and an anxious looking woman.

"According to my workings out," the woman assured the man, "Time is money, so money matters."

"Believe me, Miss Calculation," the man who called himself The Truth argued, "I am The Truth and I will take care of everything."

When they turned their attention to calculating co-ordinates for her journey, Lost Girl rolled her eyes and shlucked off through the mud, towards the biggest marquee.

Packed to the hilt with folks in bizarre costumes, the marquee was hot and heaved with human energy. At one side of the tent was a row of long trestle tables laden with huge pink cakes, their icing shiny in the heat.

"Welcome to Imagination," said a Nosy Parker who did not look at all welcoming. "Leave your predicaments at the door."

Clinging to the orange carpetbag, Lost Girl pushed past the Nosy Parker who was busy turning away the purple elf and her dog, and made her way deep into the arrhythmic, distorted noise generated by an oversized DJ with headphones on his horns. This was a tent of surprises and aunties and one thing after another confounded Lost Girl's expectations, until she abandoned all preconceptions. A Volunteer, whose job was to sweep the problem-strewn ground, winked with his one eye. She remembered her hours spent cleaning at Moose House and wondered if he felt appreciated.

At the fourteenth stroke of impossibility, she sat next to a man split in two halves from head to toe; the halves bent sideways away from each other at an alarming angle so he resembled a bunch of bananas.

"What's the idea?" asked Lost Girl when she had aligned the parts so his mouth could work properly.

"Chal-lenge" he said. "I thought my alter–native would be different, more into–resting."

"And was he?"

"No. I have two i-den-tickle lives. It is dreadfully stressful being in two places at once or the same place twice over." Lost Girl offered to pin him together with pine needles, but he upped and hopped sideways into the crowd, clutching at his trousers to stop them falling down.

Time stepped into the tent and a stray Moldavian band began to play along to the rhythm he brought with him. He was in party mood and had genuinely paid the entrance fee to the festival, although the Nosy Parker at the gate didn't seem to know what to do with the time he put on her hands. Whilst she had been conveniently distracted by a sense of being rewound like an old-fashioned cassette tape, a small scruffy dog ignored the 'Definitely no Dogs' sign and slipped through the gate.

The sound of music moved branches aside and wended its way through the Picture of the Green Green Woods to filter into the dream spaces of Snailbeach dwellers. It curled around their ears and tickled their cheeks. "Come and find me," it sang.

A musician with hair as long as her own, handed Lost Girl a guitar.

"I can't play," she complained, holding up her small hands as an excuse.

"Music is as simple as a single sound or as complex as a concept. De-jing, de-jing, thrum," he insisted, and together they picked, riffed and sang a song with as many verses as there are things to sing about.

The layers of sound lit up the festival and started small fires. Vaguely recalling another party, Lost Girl put down the guitar and abandoned herself to the crowd.

Time sat in the shadows behind a three-tiered pink cake so heavy it bowed the table. Written in icing on the pink surface of the huge bottom tier, in neat scratchy handwriting, were the words

'His Majesty the Holly King and the Honourable Bag Lady, to mark their Engagement'. Underneath, in a less distinguished hand - 'sponsored by Creative Cakes Limited'

He absentmindedly toyed with the strawberry jam and cream which had begun to squeeze out from between the layers of sponge the moment he stepped into the marquee. Watching the dancing girl with the long eagle wing feather that jutted from beneath one shoulder blade, he felt sure he had found the missing Story Book

Girl. He also recognised the figure whose toned muscles stretched his shiny green suit as he reflected the girl's every move with his body, gazing hypnotically into her eyes. The Holly King had found Story Book Girl at the festival long before Time. Nature's mood in their team meeting had been foul and she had made no secret of the fury she felt at Bag Lady's engagement to the Holly King. Now it appeared that Time had inadvertently stumbled upon his father's phony engagement party, planned to subvert all Hope – how inconvenient when he was just beginning to get into the swing of his holiday. His eyes searched the marquee for Bag Lady, but if she was at her own party, she was keeping a low profile, leaving her fiancé to disco with a tenderer family member.

Mr King smooched up beside Lost Girl, so close she could smell the cloying scent of aftershave on his neck. A golden horn (awarded for business enterprise) glinted against his chest.

"Come with me," he whispered, reaching out to touch Lost Girl in a disconcerting way she remembered from a dream, revealing a row of perfect white teeth. "I'll show you who you really are."

135

Time considered his options, which were in the region of three hundred and seventy one to the power of ten times forty seven per second; he decided that the best thing he could do without blowing his cover was to slow down the tempo and break up the party until he could get Story Book Girl out of danger.

The musicians mysteriously experienced a delay between the beat and their response. The rhythm stuttered and broke and Lost Girl faltered, aware of the rough carpetbag scratching her hot skin. "Think carefully," the scientist had warned.

When the music stopped, the General Public gathered their handbags a tad sulkily and left the marquee. Time watched in satisfaction as Lost Girl pushed past the Holly King and was submerged by the throng.

"Prickles!" blasted the furious Mr King, dashing out of the tent. "Children are so ungrateful nowadays." His muscles flexed, he drew himself up to his full height to search for any sign of the girl.

Time ducked behind a purple elf with a small scruffy dog and punched the air. Then, with one more piece of pink cake in his hand, in celebration of his minor victory against the powers of darkness, he followed Lost Girl to the third marquee.

After a heated discussion with a Nosy Parker who claimed they would be contravening health and safety regulations, the travellers settled as best they could on the rough ground and tried to sleep. Time sat on guard with his back to the entrance and looked out into the green gloom. The accountant counted steam sheep and the man who called himself The Truth prodded her in the ribs when he couldn't hear himself pray. The teenager dreamed she was laughing with her mother and woke up with a terrible allergy. All fell quiet and the woods were no more than a green picture, insubstantial and paused.

Mr King rolled up his sleeves and picked at the scabs on his arms; something he was inclined to do when his plans went awry. His ambitious business mission (approved by the manager of a once well respected high street bank) had been to STOP the earth, but human beings were racing out of control and even at his very own festival they refused to comply. More and more of the world population had become depressed by the measures he had put in place to make life uncomfortable, thereby encouraging them to buy more distractions; but contrary to his expectations, twenty-four hour shopping and non-stop internet chat had turned despondency into a ranting epidemic. That interfering liberal, Nature, hadn't helped matters by getting into a flap and employing Bag Lady, of all people, to sort things out. Surely she should have known by then that Bag Lady seldom got it right. With the ears of the forest he had heard about Story Book Girl – Nature's new hope, a beautiful love child, who would light up the world with positive thoughts.

"Pah! Big business and globilisation are the way forward and Nature needs to get real."

Admittedly, engagement to Bag Lady was a long shot, but the lonely were such easy meat and he had enjoyed her pathetic capitulation. Of course, his ultimate target was the girl, and he had been so close, but the young fool appeared to have slipped the net for now – protected wherever she went by the interminable optimists who recognised the hope she carried in her orange carpetbag.

"What's going on?" Mr King returned to the party tent to find several Nosy Parkers standing straight and close together, in front of the trestle table sporting the huge pink cake. Moving them aside with an impatient sweep of his hand, he caught sight of his engagement cake sliding from the table in a glutinous puddle of pink.

Chapter Four

In which Mouse inadvertently changes the story

Mouse left the kitchen at Moose House, where he had been examining the food cupboards with some concern. On his way to the living room he stopped in the hallway and wondered what was missing. The clock, he decided, congratulating himself on his powers of observation - the tick of the clock was missing. He looked up at the brassy face of the grandfather clock and it gave him a non-committal stare in return. Short of running up its insides, he didn't have much to do with the clock and took its tick for granted. But Mouse is a creature of habit and had developed eczema on his paw as a result of the recent upset. He would mention the missing tick to Moose.

Moose House had been so untidy since the obsessive Story Book Girl went away, and the kitchen smelled of squiggels and more recently a hint of Four Seven Eleven Eau de Cologne. Mouse continued to the living room and was greeted by piles of bills and assorted junk mail. He pondered the fact that they had all but forgotten how wonderful it had been when Story Book Girl had arrived amongst them and had even come to resent the way she cleaned and tidied all the time. Well, she wasn't here anymore, and that was that, and they couldn't go on thinking she would be back at any moment. He sniffed and blew his nose loudly on a tissue; Mouse was wise and realised that once someone had become part of your story, they could never really leave it.

He knelt down and began to sort through one of the piles – a history of electricity bills, eye care voucher, festival flyer, warranty for a toaster they no longer owned, old fashioned end of roll negative photograph with no image on it. He sighed and began a pile of things to throw away, resolutely tearing them in half so he couldn't change his mind: receipts, birthday cards, tissues, a battered map...

Ignoring the arrows that insisted they proceed in an orderly fashion from left to right, Lost Girl and her fellow travellers bobbed along beside the river, trusting its inexorable journey to the sea. They kept an eye out for clues to their stories and every time they reached a fork in the path, alternative possibilities lay just out of sight. Under the surface of every step was a world of shifting emotion and the juxtaposition of place and occasion for each and every one of them. When she ran away they always caught up and there was usually another version of The Truth upon their heels, demanding some attention.

Time had settled into a steady rhythm behind and to one side of the travellers, he went neither slowly or fast and as he was wafer thin and one dimensional he couldn't be detected by the human eye. He had unfortunately developed an inner ear disturbance as a result of travelling in no particular direction, and reflected, with a hint of nostalgia, that in his normal working day the past lay behind, fixed and immutable, whilst the future lay ahead with unknown challenges.

Time was still, strictly speaking, on holiday, but his influence on the hill was undeniable. All around the festival field, people whispered between themselves about things they may do in the future and Nosy Parkers issued parking tickets to people who stood still for too long. Mr King, his arms a mass of sticking plasters, searched high and low for Story Book Girl and issued an edict forbidding anyone (except that confounded dog) to enter or leave the festival.

Chapter Five

In which Story Book Girl hitches a lift.

In a story, a miniscule turn in any direction will present different prospects entirely. As Mouse tore Bag Lady's map in two, a crack appeared and the travellers glimpsed beyond the Picture of the Green Green Woods. Time's heart skipped a beat as he realised he was the only one of his team who knew that Lost Girl was about to leave the wood.

The Truth struck her and her footsteps faltered.

"Ouch!" Everyone stopped in their tracks and looked around at each other. "This is ridiculous. Why must I go any further?"

"It's a bit late for that now," said the man who called himself The Truth, whose feet were suffering due to entirely inappropriate footwear, "We didn't start this nonsense. I, for instance, was quite happy at the festival, eating cake."

"Me too, I was hap-pea," lied Banana man, once he had got his act together and fastened his fly.

"Oh, do be quiet," retorted Lost Girl, exasperated at how soon they had forgotten that they were the ones who had followed her. "I'm trying to decide what I should be doing."

"According to my reckoning, what you should be doing is always what you are doing," advised the accountant.

"And what is that?" asked Lost Girl.

Through some kind of unacknowledged affection for Nature and an even greater dislike of the Holly King, his own father, Time had already made the decision to put his holiday on hold until this mess was sorted out and Story Book Girl was returned to Moose House. Okay, enough of the green half light and annoying drizzle; Time had a few tricks and a lot of experience to draw upon. He smiled to himself and making full use of the power vested in him by Nature, he authorised a new dawn.

Out of the sunrise came a seventeen ton blue lorry.

Phizz, Bang, Blink - it came to a halt as it reached Lost Girl and the driver slid across to the nearside of the cab.

"Hi, I'm Bear," announced the small furry driver, through the open window. "Any idea how to fix this back on?" She pointed to the wing mirror, which hung at a jaunty angle.

Between them, Bear and Lost Girl managed a temporary mend and stood back to admire their work.

Bear looked in the mirror and waved at Time, who gave her the thumbs up. "Please climb aboard," she urged Lost Girl, with a big smile, struggling to be heard against the grumble of the engine. "I know which direction you are travelling in and I can take you some of the way. Besides, the company would be good."

Lost Girl looked back at her companions, still arguing amongst themselves, and in the light of the new morning knew that, like the river, she must continue her journey.

Nodding, she hurled her carpetbag onto the front seat, took the paw that was offered and clambered up beside Bear in the cab. The travellers shuffled about and were about to climb in beside Lost Girl until she looked at them daggers. Moaning, they slunk around the side of the lorry to the metal door that clanked as it bent in the middle and opened to let in its new guests. Still moaning, they pulled themselves up one by one, and settled down for the ride like seasoned refugees.

"I have some clothes for you." Bear pointed to an orange garment made of finest silk, and a pair of dainty sandals, which hung in the cab as if she had been expected.

Lost Girl looked at Bear and thought she recognised the eyes and the big smile of her companion from a photograph on a shelf in Snailbeach. She couldn't recall exactly where the shelf had been, but was grateful for the lift.

Bear released the hydraulic brakes and shifted the gear stick, which grated into position. Soon they were laughing and singing along to "These Boots are Made for Walking", sharing memories Lost Girl didn't know she had and travelling cross country, alongside the River Onny, lit by a radiance which may have been sunshine.

Where will the river go? To the West and Onny slow,

past Bog and Castle, Hill and Rhadley,

Linley, More, meandering madly,

Eaton, Myndmill on past Plowden

through the valleys, down and round them,

past Glenburrell, Cheney Longville

nestling safe below the big hill,

Craven Arms and Onibury

gathering speed and in a hurrry

Ludlow, Overton, Ashford Carbonell

Little Hereford, Berrington, Tenbury Wells,

awash in Eastham, Stanford Bridge,

cutting jagged rock and ridge,

Ankerdine Hill and Derbys Green

always there, not always seen,

Broadwas, Leigh, Rushwick, Powys Hams

to meet the Severn, here it slams and makes its mark,

widening, thickening, green and dark

Kempsey, Clevelode, Rhydd, Holdfast,

waved at Tewkesbury as it passed

Chaceley Stock and Apperley Gloucester, Bollow, Eppley

Framilode and onto Priding, along to Strand,

The river widening, Westbury, Newnham, Awre and Purton

washed along a water curtain,

Sharpness, Newtown, place called Lydney

hold my hand and drop down quickly,

further on to Alvington broaden out at Tidenham,

Oldbury, Littleton, Beachley, Aust,

Severn Beach, Avonmouth, Portishead and Redcliff Bay

waves wash and fish play at Goldcliff, Clevedon, Western Super-Mare

sand on its feet and salt in its hair.

"How long is my story?" asked Lost Girl as their conversation curled around the lorry like a water snake.

"Before humans began to think they might be able to live for ever, it used to be said that a human story was three score years and ten. But I don't think our stories begin when we are born; neither do they end when we die; it is more complex than that." Bear crunched through the gears. "Perhaps the story is here already, waiting for us to be a part of it. But our part is not linear or chronological.

147

We are ingredients, bowl tipped and spoon stirred, and once we enter into the mix, nothing will ever be the same again."

Somewhere along the road, they reached the subject of the sea.

"What is the sea, Bear?"

"There is only so far we can get on our own two feet," said Bear. "Sometimes we need the pull of lunar tides."

"Go further? But I'm tired." Lost Girl tried to remember where she was meant to be going. Somewhere on the long road she had begun to feel safe in the care of her new friend and tears coursed down her cheeks at the thought of their parting.

"I can't carry you any further," replied Bear. "I have other journeys to make, to places which you are not ready to visit."

They had arrived at a port with small white boats and an ocean the colour of lapis lazuli.

"This is where you go it alone. We all have to do it sooner or later," said Bear. "But I have a gift for you."

She opened her door, jumped down onto the road and swung her furry frame into the back of the lorry. Lost Girl watched her for a moment through the giant wing mirror, then grabbed the heavy orange carpetbag and scrambled to follow, curious about the lorry's cargo. The door at one side of the vehicle was reached by a steep step, through which could be seen rich wood cladding and pretty lanterns. There was a black wood stove with a chimney, and strong smells of burnt oak, cinnamon and marshmallows hung in the air. The travellers were sitting on embroidered cushions or lying comfortably on handmade quilts and blankets inside the lorry, and with them sat a medley of ancestors, entertained by the antics of the newcomers. Tell-tale homemade biscuit crumbs fell to the floor as the man who called himself The Truth stood up respectfully, but none of them made any move to get out of the lorry.

Bear came to the step and held out her paw for the second time. "Don't be afraid to trust kindnesses, and believe in the power of friendship," she said, clasping Lost Girl's hand. "Please accept my gift – when it is time, you will understand."

Lost Girl felt a sharp pain in the palm of her hand.

"What about the others?" Lost Girl looked over Bear's shoulder at her fellow travellers who were so wrapped in debate they hardly noticed her.

"Each of us has our own story," replied Bear, smiling as she climbed down the steps and closed the door. "There are moments when we dance past each other and glimpse ourselves in someone else's eyes, but then the moment is gone and we move on again."

Lost Girl stepped back and the small bear returned to the cab.

Phizz, Bang, Blink - the hydraulic brakes hissed as the giant lorry moved off, and a paw waved out of the window.

Chapter Six

In which Bag Lady gets a nasty shock and a dog

During her brief liaison with the Holly King, it had almost been possible to believe in a happy ending for herself. As she dabbed her wrists with a little Four Seven Eleven cologne and put on a ridiculously large pair of rose-tinted spectacles, given to her as an engagement present by a fairy with crinkly blonde hair, her spirits lifted. Not wishing to arrive late at her own engagement party, she checked the clock in the hall at Moose House but couldn't hear it ticking. Blaming the over-production of earwax, she trusted her instincts and left the house in what she thought was good time. She used the back door to avoid the attention of the police officer waiting in his car near the front of the house to arrest her for suspected poisoning, kidnap and possibly murder.

"Easy does it," she chuckled as she dragged her carrier bags on up the hill, smiling toothlessly at the woman from Radio Shropshire who was speaking animatedly to her dictaphone, while pointing at the twenty or so cars parked at the village hall, all of which seemed to have been issued with parking tickets. Reaching the woods, Bag Lady turned three hundred and sixty degrees in order to check she was alone, and spoke an incantation learned from her fiancé, Mr King.

The woods shifted subtly and the light changed; the air grew heavy and closed around her like a cloak. Directly in front of her, there appeared a wooden gate.

"I'm sorry, we're full," came an abrupt voice from the other side.

For the second time that day, Bag Lady thought she hadn't heard properly.

"I don't think you understand, this is my..."

"Oh, I understand perfectly, duck," retorted the red faced Nosy Parker. "But if we let everyone in, there would be no-one anywhere else. I have strict instructions, pet, *strict* instructions."

Bag Lady could have argued; anger rose in her belly and her mouth fell open as if she was about to speak. But the habits of a lifetime do not change in a moment. With a gulp which saved her lungs from collapsing, she internalised her disappointment and suffered, instead, a huge 'ah ping' moment –

How could she have been so stupid?

How could she have believed in her wildest dreams that any one could love her?

Removing the rose-tinted glasses with difficulty, resulting in the loss of the top of her left ear, Bag Lady went to sit under a tree to consider her options and was further dismayed to find that the ground was covered with a layer of pink, sticky stuff oozing from beneath the festival gate. It wasn't long before she heard cross tones and realised that someone else was getting evicted from the festival.

"No dogs allowed! Can't you read?" The Nosy Parker pointed at a sign nailed to the gate.

The Purple Elf remonstrated. "But I keep telling you, he's not my dog, he just turned up and started following me about. I need to find out who he belongs to."

"Tough!" The Nosy Parker bent down to pick up the animal.

"Excuse me, er, hello." The Purple Elf looked at Bag Lady, appealing for help.

Despite Bag Lady's preoccupation, the curiosity that had shaped her life made her look up at the elf, whom she thought she might have met before.

"I have to go back to the festival, you see. There are so many lost people in there and I have to help them find their stories."

Bag Lady looked with dull eyes at the elf, whom she was now sure she recognised, and said nothing, though she knew what was being asked. Painfully, she struggled to her feet and faced the Nosy Parker.

"The dog. Now!" she said, holding out her newspaper arms.

Caught off guard, the Nosy Parker dropped the bemused dog onto the ground at Bag Lady's feet and disappeared back into the festival, clicking his tongue and the gate as he went. The bontiful Purple Elf hung around for a while, but Bag Lady clearly wasn't interested in gratitude. Finally the elf turned on her heel.

"Well Dog, it looks like it's just you and me."

Dog stopped licking the pink icing from the pads of his feet, growled and backed away. He glanced at the gate, then jumped and ran sideways as a sudden wind rustled Bag Lady's carrier bags.

Bag Lady looked around and shivered, then she picked up the bags and made a poor attempt at a whistle. "Come on, Dog. The Green Green Wood is no place to be in a storm."

Nature was at her wits' end. In an attempt to cure a drought in Australia, she had accidently flooded China; the tabloids were having a field day, blaming her for every disaster on the planet, and her small team had apparently disintegrated, leaving her to abandon any real strategy and thrash about like a landed fish. She watched as human beings switched their political allegiances and the world economy sunk into depression, then she locked her office from the outside and hung a sign on the door – 'Gone to Lunch'.

Returning in a distracted state from the Picture of the Green Green Woods, with Dog walking a few paces behind her, Bag Lady had forgotten to avoid the front of Moose House, and on arrival the 'witch' and 'her familiar' were arrested immediately. Ross, the young uniformed officer from Bishop's Castle, who seldom had to deal with more than a broken window, was very excited on the drive to Pontesbury Police Station. He advised the officer on duty of the severity of the charges against her and Bag Lady was treated to seventy-two hours in the only cell, whilst Dog, who seemed an innocent sort after all, was provided with a blanket and given best lamb, bought at Hignetts of Pontesbury. Finding no evidence to charge her under the Prevention of Terrorism Act, they returned Bag Lady's belongings and released her with a shake of the head. There was a last minute debate about the status of the dog, as he clearly did not belong to or have any love for the old witch, and neither was he micro-chipped.

"We have decided that the dog should be confiscated, madam," said the unhappy police officer, who had been hoping things would escalate further during his shift than to the matter of a confiscated dog.

Bag Lady considered Dog with something that might have been affection on a more mobile face.

"Everything happens for a reason in stories, Dog," she explained.

Dog made as if he had heard nothing and Bag Lady wasn't in the mood for cajoling. Without a backward glance, she left the police station, caught the last bus to Plox Green and hobbled up the hill to Moose House.

Moose was not exactly welcoming. There was no doubt in his mind that Bag Lady had something to do with the disappearance of Story Book Girl. He only went to the door because he thought Ray had returned from the Stiperstones Inn, where he sat, watched over by the great Eagle, whenever he wasn't mindlessly moving computer chess pieces. Moose stood well back as the eyes he had never liked to look upon peered up through the letterbox and she tried to persuade him that if he let her back in she would sort everything out.

"Moooo!" mooed Moose when he finally consented to open the door a crack in order for them to talk more easily.

Moose and Bag Lady stared at each other hard.

"A few hours, dear Moose, and I will be out of your antlers."

Without waiting for his decision, Bag Lady picked up her carrier bags and squeezed past Moose's legs before he could close the door. Moose wondered at what point his story had become so complicated.

As unusually fierce storms raged into their fourth night, Bag Lady studied Moose's wooden hourglass, its graceful shape representing the present as a fleeting moment that so easily could be snapped, leaving no path from the past into the future. She had tried to knit, but whatever stitch she attempted, her wool tangled.

"I just have to find out where she has wandered to and bring her home."

She rifled through Moose's 'to do' piles in an attempt to find the ordnance survey map she had prepared so carefully. It was a shame the silly girl had forgotten to take it with her, but if only she could find it, she would be able to set things straight. Failing to find it, with a sigh that sent the dust bunnies running for cover, she shuffled through the kitchen and taking the doorknob from her pocket, let herself into the forbidden place. It was time to continue the story she had begun.

Back and forth across the ages she had travelled. Sent to rescue an English village from 16th century plague, she had used a toxic concoction of herbs stolen from a dead villager's garden. The story, never written, embedded itself in the stone walls of the church and in the bones buried there. She crossed history and culture, attempting to make things right, then wrote it all down in her big black book. Ah yes, she had lived in many a place - a mud hut here, a garden shed there; once she had shared her room with a beaver and for a time she had lived in a cave with a grizzly bear. This time, her resting place was the suite of rooms at the back of Moose House, where the clothes got dirty and then got clean; where the coal store stood next to the washing machine.

For a while, it had felt as if there would never again be the need for her involvement in other people's stories; that she would have one all of her own. She had imagined life with Mr King – eternal winter solstice and no need for a show of optimism – and had been determined to embrace her new beginning with renewed conviction.

Now, she resigned herself to being the one who witnessed happiness and despair and recorded the stories so that others might learn from them. She leaned back against the kitchen chair, grimacing with the keen pain of arthritis that made her aware of her failing human form, and put her gnarled newspaper hands behind her head. Her fingers read the thinness of her coarse grey hair and the flaking skin beneath it. She was an ancient crone and the constant travelling from story to story had left its inky marks on her body and soul.

It was a shame that the others at Moose House seemed to have taken Story Book Girl's disappearance so badly, but Bag Lady was used to being unpopular. She had known from the start that her stay in Snailbeach was destined to be temporary; her task to plait the pieces of a tale into the perfect firelighter; a tale so strange and wonderful that Shropshire storytellers would nestle it deep in their hearts and use it to ignite imaginations in dark places, where a tiny spark can comfort and grow. The world would move on and Bag Lady would be scrambled from memory, supplanted by younger, more entertaining company, until she was needed again. Perhaps it was time to put aside her own interests and find a way to reunite Ray and Story Book Girl so that everyone could live happily ever after?

Bag Lady sat down at a big old computer that, with a bit of jiggery pokery, she had fixed up – just about. The computer was a good-tempered sort who was glad to be back in service – and this magic was easy. Whatever she wrote, would happen, she just had to… She closed her paper eyelids, wiped her grizzled newspaper nose on the sleeve of her tunic and rested her twisted hands on the keyboard. Back bent, so her arms did not have to straighten, she lost herself in words. Her breath rasped and spasmed, but she was content as the story unravelled and revealed itself. Electricity lit up the hills, a diorama offered itself to the back of her cloudy ricepaper eyes and words appeared on the screen.

Tap tap tap.

Chapter Seven

In which Lost Girl reaches the sea, but categorically not Western-Super-Mare

Lost Girl gazed in wonder at the vastness of the sea. She was pretty sure, judging by the weather, she was not in Western-Super-Mare. She picked up her orange carpetbag and walked towards life.

Life was in the small shops carrying gifts of the sea: bright terracotta pots, furry toy turtles and authentic Greek playing cards; in the pretty tavernas with their mixture of unconcerned lassitude and raw competitiveness; in the sun-hot metal machinery which brought soft golden sand to a hot seaside aspiring to be a cool paradise.

She approached a man of thin clothing, peggy teeth and balding head and asked him the price of hiring a boat. He insisted, she haggled and they shook on it, even though Lost Girl knew very well that she did not have any money. He glanced at the cross and circle tattooed on the palm of her hand and showed her to a plastic table at which they sat on uncomfortable plastic chairs. She kicked off the embroidered flip flops given to her by Bear, and tucked her feet underneath her on the chair. He, full of self-importance, brought out a folder of almost unintelligible paperwork and pointed out the rules and regulations pertaining to the hire of a boat. Taking his pen, she scratched her signature upon the contract he proffered. He looked at the name she wrote and presumed it to be from a country he had no knowledge of, save from an annual airing as part of the Eurovision Song Contest.

Reaching inside the orange carpetbag, she took out the periodic table; unfolded it and held it out to the man. She explained to him that he must close his eyes and choose a square. Understanding or not, the man was intrigued by the seductive green eyes and indefinable magnetism of his customer. He spread the crinkled paper on the table at which they sat and made a mischievous play of divining the right spot with a magic finger. 79, he chose, as she had known he would. 79 - the number of gold. Mimicking his magic show, she elaborately placed her palms over the numbered square. She picked up the seventy-nine gold pieces that materialised on the table, and handed them to the man. He looked across at her with narrowed eyes – a little scared, she thought with some satisfaction.

She laughed disarmingly and reminded him that he owed her change. He walked back to his tavern. Lost Girl wondered whether he would still be working there in the morning, having made a fortune beyond a lifetime's wages. He returned with two small glasses of Ouzo.

"In celebration," he said, breaking into a smile at last.

"Steen eeyiasas!" she adjoined, and raised her glass to his, then downed the anise flavoured drink with one swift movement, shuddering. She glanced towards the line where the sand slid beneath the sea.

The boats were lazily bobbing against the jetty, but what caught her eye was the beautiful man who stood bare-chested upon the sand, sunglasses holding golden brown hair back from his forehead. Thanking the boat man, Lost Girl put the periodic table back in her bag and stood up, straightening her orange shift and slipping her feet into pretty shoes.

In port, I thought I recognised Van Vorhead.
We cruised the bars, spoke in whispers, smoked and
giggled.
He winked an eye and I paid the price.

Once aboard, eyes tight shut against the push of
unfamiliar water,
he taught me to drift, with some blinded intent;
to sail my boat in unknown seas.

We steer oceanward, on a whim;
over seas of exquisite beauty;
charting our progress by the sonar of love and the width of
smiles.

Decked, when he is asleep,
I clamber to the nest of crows,
and dare to peep between dream stained fingers.

Observe gruesome, tentacled monsters
yawning at the bow;
splintered flotsam crashing
at the heels of my leaking vessel;
The last oil............   slick;
a drowning girl mirrored in dark waters;
albatross dead upon the boards.

Eyes closed,
I curl around him, unanchored,
and the sun rises.

Chapter Eight

In which Van Vorhead is strangely familiar and Lost Girl becomes Bird Girl

Van Vorhead rubbed heavy eyelids with the back of a fist. He stretched out long legs like a sun-blissed ferret and turned away from the light with a frown, attempting to shrink back into a night-time place of honour without responsibility. Vaguely, he became conscious of sea-wet kisses, licking him awake gently with a rough, teasing tongue. He opened one sleep-bruised eye and was greeted with the meow of the ship's cat, Withpy, a pretty, nervous moggy with black and white fur as fine as fairy needles.

The tawny coloured captain gradually became aware of other sounds as his vessel 'Truth', pierced the water with sinuous limbs, splintering its bow imperceptibly to realign strong supporting boards as it pushed into the new sunlight and another day's adventure. He uncurled the fist and reached for the bottle habitually at his side. Manoeuvring onto an elbow, he carelessly tipped elderberry liquor onto lips and beard and massaged it into his gums. Head aching, he lay back for a moment, rubbing his temple to dissipate the familiar tightness.

Van Vorhead stumbled to his feet, struggling to find sea legs that sometimes were so strong and sure. He searched the array of strewn garments for something that had been his, and wondered to whom the scanty lace lingerie could belong. Pulling on crumpled jeans, ripped at the knee, he ducked, but banged his head upon the door lintel anyway, and left cabin for deck, a colourful ball of fingerknitting clasped in his leathery brown hand.

Through blurred eyes he first saw the girl who had always been in his dreams. She stood with her back to him, the other end of the wool in her hand, staring out across the turquoise Adriatic Sea. Her skimpy orange shift blew in the breeze so that the top half of her body resembled a startling, orange bird of paradise about to embark on a whimsical flight.

"But," considered Van Vorhead, "the legs are solid, the hips are real and the waist is a familiar, comfortable place for a man to slide his arms around."

Van Vorhead felt every inch a man, though his temple ached and his hands shook.

"Huh Hum," he coughed, moving close enough to be heard by the Bird Girl without shocking her into flight.

"Bonjour," he tried again, with a dodgy cockney accent.

She turned around and her green eyes undressed him. She laughed. "The Captain is up early this morning."

Van Vorhead glanced up at the sun to ascertain the hour. "So what's the plan?"

163

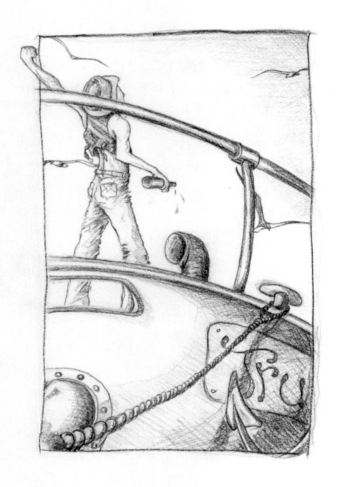

The effervescent orange bird stepped up and span around him so before he knew it his legs were tied together with brightly coloured wool. Still off balance, he made a clumsy attempt to pull free and found himself floundering on the deck of his vessel, giggling uncontrollably.

Some time later, Bird Girl and Van Vorhead contemplated a map of blue and gold and plotted their adventure. Van Vorhead was a self-proclaimed, experienced sea cowboy and his voice took on a lilt as he told tales of scabby pirates, gleaming treasure and monsters of the deep. Occasionally, he tipped his one hundred percent paper cowboy hat at a jaunty angle and glanced sideways to check whether Bird Girl appreciated his tall tales and fiddle faddle.

"It was that big!" he gesticulated.

The landing of a mermaid stretched her imagination to a point where she laughed and snorted out loud. He picked her up unceremoniously and dipped her feathered head in the wavelets that lapped the boat.

They travelled along the south coast of Kefalonia, stopping to explore desecrated monasteries and deserted beaches. When the earth grew fiery and they could no longer stand upon the scorching white-pebbled beach, they evicted bell-bedecked goats from a shallow cave and rested there through the 'dead time', their heads close together. Van Vorhead began a snoring fest, drifting off to watery places, fathoms deep. Bird Girl perched in her colourful dreamscape and peered out to sea, sharp eyes moving between boat and horizon, for no-one could travel through the sudden sea mists that came from nowhere and hung like cataracts across an artist's eyes.

When there was nothing to drink on the boat, they plundered coffee shops, demanding Nescafé and chewing on mouth-watering coconut sticks, served by somnambulistic locals who seemed puzzled to find themselves running a café. Bird Girl felt guilty at first: wanting, enjoying, stealing and running, until she spotted Van Vorhead paying a bill in secret, with a wink of the eye and a manly handshake, before urging her to 'run for it', following her with whooping cries and gambols, across white pebbles and into the bay. In low afternoon, as life began to pour back into Katelios and Porthos, they returned to the vessel, casting their fishing lines into the deep, translucent sea and waiting patiently for a bright eyed sea bass, wrass or bream to take the bait. Van Vorhead's blue eyes flashed as he heaved his catch aboard.

"Get the net. The net!" he demanded.

Bird Girl hissed at being given an order, but there was something exciting about being compelled, pushed, and she bit back the vitriolic reaction, swooping to his side with an appreciative grunt.

He turned to measure her with those eyes, leaning back to laugh out loud before sliding close to show her the fish clutched in his scarred fingers. They breathed each other in and for a precious moment, they were quiet.

Van Vorhead boasted of his great prowess as a fisherman and protested that they would never be able to eat the whole catch. They fed each other with the soft, white flesh and Withpy cleared the deck of scraps and bones before the moon rose and they sat in abeyance, whilst Captain Corelli's turtles turned into discarded cookie packets and nodded as they passed by on their journey along the coast.

Van Vorhead switched easily between bottles as the evening progressed, so dropping anchor was a fumbled affair. They rubbed their feet together to make fire, and doused themselves in enough citronella to tickle the noses of the most persistent mosquitoes, before singing songs with alternative words and eccentric tunes and dancing until they fell over in a tangle of fingerknitting and laughter.

Once, when they had nothing pressing to do except sail the boat, Van Vorhead asked Bird Girl where she came from.

"I was born out of flames," she offered mysteriously, cocking her head to one side as if considering her own answer, and sheltering her scantily clad body beneath Van Vorhead's free arm. He tossed his head in mock annoyance and playfully bit her shoulder. She was stronger than he thought and tugged his hair until he broke free and concentrated his gaze on the distant horizon, surreptitiously rubbing his scalp.

"And who are you?" she tempted after a while.

"I don't want to talk about it," he pouted.

"That's fine."

"My name is Van Vorhead," he began with a flourish. "I sailed from Holland in 1667, in Blauwe Arent, a Dutch vessel of beauty and renown. The floor was flat, the bilge was square and she stood rakish in the water, like so." He held his arms up to the front of him and tipped his head back so his bearded chin struck out proudly.

"Her gilded stern was hung with bright lanterns and the passage of our hours at sea was marked by bells. She carried royalty and she carried me and we crossed to England in the night."

"16...?"

But the only answer was Van Vorhead's loud singing as he developed and embellished his latest ditty, occasionally wiping spittle from his three hundred-year-old moustache.

That night, the wine bottles emptied steadily and he ranted about the toxic state of the seabed and the refusal of the Mer King's Water Board to take action. "Someone responsible ought to be in charge," he raved, painting the night sky with his bottle.

Bird Girl wasn't listening. She watched as the sea changed, became agitated, restless. The familiar sea mists began their roll towards the boat, landmarks in the middle distance already indistinct.

Van Vorhead failed to register anything atmospheric, supposing the blear was an inconvenient side effect of being delightfully drunk. He reached out towards the Bird Girl he thought would taste the best and lost his purchase on the wet boards.

His companion drew her eyes from the fermenting water and finding a new strength in her upper body, dragged the unconscious sailor to a place below the deck. Too alarmed to be irritated, she used her superior eyesight and balance to find her way back to the helm. Their only chance was to sail straight through the mist towards land, in the hope that the rocks lay deep enough to allow them safe anchorage.

Chapter Nine

In which Mouse and Shy Mouse build a movie camera

There are worlds that can only be imagined through a box and a mirror. Mouse and Shy Mouse of Stiperstones discovered this when they adventured into film-making.

Mouse had been tetchy of late and anyway, his teeth hurt; there hadn't been any decent cereal in the house for weeks. Since Story Book Girl left, Moose House had been engulfed by a black cloud and sometimes, when he pattered from room to room, he almost caught the furniture whispering darkly. Moose didn't seem to want to talk about it, so Mouse sought the cheerful company of his friend, Shy Mouse.

Recently, Shy Mouse had discovered that by climbing into the bread bin and peering out through a crack in the side, he could see the world from a different perspective: human beings looked smaller, more comical than threatening, and greater height opened up new vistas, the possibility of new relationships and cupboards full of food. He mulled over his new experience and concluded that by altering the way we look at things, we can actually bring about real change.

He talked about his discovery to his story makers but they seemed a bit vague in their understanding:

"Yes, Shy Mouse, sounds verrrrrry interesting, but dinner's in the oven," – that kind of thing.

So Shy Mouse waited until they were in a creative space and concentrated hard until they reinvented him slightly and gave him a new, important role to play that would demonstrate his theory.

Being a generous and enthusiastic soul, he dispatched Boingy, the slightly eccentric post-bird blue tit, to Moose house at seven thirty one Sunday morning to deliver a mousage.

Boingy thrust her feathery chest at the upstairs window having twice banged her head on the eaves.

"Tweet – bring your stuff. Tweet – some kind of box and something to stick it with. Also things to make a camera work – Tweet. We're going to make a film!"

Mouse is not an early starter, so at first he was cross with Boingy.

"!!!"

"Oi – Tweet, don't shoot the messenger. Only doin' me job – TWEET!"

As usual, when he went on an adventure, Mouse packed his turquoise case and by eight o'clock he was making his way carefully down the treacherous garden path (there are many things that poke a mouse's eye just for the fun of it).

The suitcase made an awful racket as its wheels hit the hard, pongo encrusted yard.

"Ow>>>grumblerumblerumble>>>Ugh>>>Ow>>>."

Mouse turned left out of the gate and prepared himself for a frustrating trip. First he must visit Farmer Lama, who had started a bus service between Snailbeach and Stiperstones. As Mouse negotiated the sizeable farmyard potholes, his case got caught on the edges and threatened to drag him down into the depths of the earth.

"Barely room for a mouse with a suitcase," he muttered.

Eventually, he reached the bus and sighed as he considered its steps; they might have worked for a person over the height of four feet, but the trajectory for a wee mouse with a suitcase was impossumably steep.

He complained loudly that he had discussed the issue with Moose (a humungous beast who found it difficult to empathize and impossible for other reasons to get on a bus) but that Moose had failed to pass the matter back to Farmer Lama, who regarded Moose as akin to an escapee cow and might not have responded favourably. Luckily, a fellow passenger noticed Mouse's struggle and helped him up and into a seat. The bus wound through the hills past Lordshill, Snailbeach Village Hall and Crow's Nest Dingle and drew to a halt outside Stiperstones School, seat of education for young children and other assorted animals. With a bit of assistance (eye popping and humiliating), Mouse alighted alongside the other passengers and crossed the road to reach Coronation Cottages, where Shy Mouse scratched out a living.

Shy Mouse lived in a house made of stories and muffins. He was conceived by two story tellers in love and, to tell you the truth, despite his name he was not one bit shy. They had built his character bit by bit over eleven years and he still wasn't finished. Sometimes, they shaded his nose differently and it had a disturbing effect on his voice. His whiskers

171

grew and retracted too, and on this occasion he tripped over them as he ran to answer the door.

"Bother."

"Oops, um hello."

"Did you get the stuff?"

"Stuff?"

"Y' know, the camera stuff?"

"Bits and pieces, odds and ends – can I come in?"

"Course y' can."

Mouse rumbled across the kitchen floor with his case and Shy Mouse helped him up onto the table with it. Together, they opened and emptied its secret places and it giggled and puckered, enjoying the attention. Mouse mentally catalogued the items:

Two rubber circles from a puncture repair kit, one mirror

fixing, one compact mirror, a broken torch, five assorted screws, one cardboard box, three curtain hooks, an old boot, an ancient pair of eye-glasses, a cut throat razor and a cork.

There had been a lot of other things in Moose's secret drawer, but Mouse had thought better of bringing them out into the open.

Shy Mouse provided paper and paints and the two meese busied themselves. Pretty soon they came up with an impressive design and high fived vigorously in a mouse sort of way.

"Sorted."

"Yay."

"Will it work?"

"Don't know – yeah."

"What now?"

"Make it."

"Make it?"

"Spect."

"Screw."

"Yup."

"Mirror."

"Yup."

"Cardboard box."

"Yup."

"Cork."

The two mice spent a happy morning assembling their prototype movie camera, with only minor skirmishes. In another time, place and story it would never have worked, but when Shy Mouse asked Mouse to pose and pronounce, "I am a dangerous terrorist!" and holding the camera up to his eye, he said, "Camera rolling – action!" they were both more than a little surprised to hear the contraption whir into life, capturing Mouse on film as he got too near the edge of the table and crashed onto the floor with his feet waving in the air (don't believe all that stuff about mice always landing on their feet). After grumpy Mouse had recovered from his fall and untangled his legs, the tiny wizards packed the movie camera in the smug turquoise suitcase and Shy Mouse led the way out of the door and across the road to the hills.

Damp, green alder leaves, hawthorn prickles, sycamore noises, rowan feathers and silver birch. Mouse fairly bounced along, a spring in his step despite misty weather and the long climb ahead. His usual trepidation at the beginning of a Shy Mouse Enterprises project had been set aside. The world opened its lips and the mice climbed inside and were carried on a wave of exuberance.

The path was steep and their legs were short, so it was a while before they reached the healer's turfed house for a mouth-scorching cuppa tea at her hearth, and after four o'clock in the afternoon when they pawsed to find a way past the wooden bar gate that opened to 'the wilderness'. They passed the broken remains of small dry stone houses built long ago by those who enclosed small plots of land and supplemented their living with the growing of vegetables and the rearing of sheep. The land was raggedy, the track straggly and a fine, wetting rain fed the rivulets that trickled down from the hills, dragging loose stones from their temporary homes.

The wizards filmed each other climbing through an old drainpipe and sliding down the hillside made muddy and exciting by the blustery squalls that characterise the weather at this time of year in that kind of place. They chatted to the sheep who still inhabited the place of their ancestors, and who were indignant at the prospect of appearing as unpaid extras in a handshot film until they were persuaded by Shy Mouse's easy charm that they would not be fleeced. Mouse stood back, a little embarrassed by Shy Mouse's quick knit wit and aware that sheep have hard heads and seem prepared to use them.

Slowly, slowly, the path below them grew longer and the summit of Stiperstones hill bent down towards the two little mice.

"Come on, Mouse," urged Shy Mouse, with a glance towards the darkening sky. "This is our big chance to make it in the movies."

Chapter Ten
In which Mouse is cajoled

"Are you crazy?"

"Possibly I am. It has been said."

"Me climb up there?"

"It would make a nice shot – look through here." Shy Mouse handed over the camera so that Mouse could see The Devil's Chair through the viewfinder. The outcrop of grey quartzite cast its shadow upon the ridge they had struggled up to that afternoon. Mouse had spent some time licking his poor sensitive feet to salve cuts caused by the numerous rocky intrusions that cannot be avoided towards the top of the crag.

"But not strictly necessary."

"Well, no, but you see my point."

"You want me to climb to the top of The Devil's Chair so you can get a dramatic shot of the dangerous terrorist falling to his death from a rock five hundred and thirty metres above sea level?"

"I think that would be cool."

"Could we just have a *little* health and safety check here?"

"Oh, come on, Mouse, you must admit, your legs are so short you are pretty near the ground anyway – hardly anywhere to fall."

"Shy Mouse, your charm is legendary."

"Appreciated. So?"

Mouse kicked a loose stone and watched it bounce away, down towards where they had come from. It had taken the two wizards most of the afternoon to get to the top of the Stiperstones and mice get overtired quite quickly, so Mouse was no longer feeling quite so keen on this whole film thing. Still, they had got some panoramic shots of the hills and a few gruesome shots of fake blood oozing from fatal wounds on wanted terrorists, so the day had not been wasted. Reluctantly, Mouse set off on his lonely ascent, occasionally stopping to wonder why it was always him who had to get a killing, whilst Shy Mouse was the hero, time and time again. But on reflection he did die rather nicely, so he decided to take it as a compliment.

Sighing with the inevitability of it all, Mouse blew his button nose on an old tissue and searched for somewhere to put it. He wished he had brought his precious suitcase with him, but Shy Mouse had wanted somewhere to rest the camera and the suitcase had not wanted to climb to the top of the hill anyway. All Mouse had with him, in fact, was a notebook, a felt tip pen and a small cube of seventy percent cocoa, FairTrade chocolate. He had hastily drawn some cue signs that Shy Mouse had said would help them to communicate when Mouse reached the summit of the Devil's Chair. Shy Mouse was filming from out of earshot, far below.

Mouse nervously picked at the corners of his tissue and put it between the pages of his notebook; Eagle didn't allow anyone to drop litter on the hills – and Eagle might pluck someone's eyes out rather than be disobeyed.

As he progressed further along the stony path, he found himself keening and mewling quietly to himself. He was full of regret at having begun this climb, and he wished beyond all wishes for the company of the great Eagle and the mighty Moose. At first, he could hear the shouted directions of Shy Mouse, who was frustrated in his attempts to balance the camera on the obstreperous suitcase to achieve the optimum shot of the Devil's Chair.

"Bother and Braces."

"Dip Wit and Bandages."

"Carrots and Cabbages."

Then he just walked, tipping his head forwards so that he could not see how far he had to travel – the sharp autumn wind at this altitude putting tears in his eyes and blowing his whiskers back against his face until it stung.

Chapter Eleven

The Devil's Story

The Devil had a vested interest in Stiperstones. It is not that the people living below the hill misbehave in any great ungodly way, but the great mines they have dug beneath the earth since the times the Romans walked the hills; the sharp twang of pick, rasp of shovel, more recently the machinery that changed the landscape, produced a resonance. This sympathetic vibration woke and rang in the heart of a troubled being who has been much maligned and surely made a scapegoat of, and who had subsequently squatted beneath these very hills, sad and a little lazy maybe, for many thousands of years. Through his dreaming, he became aware of the music of men, women and children as they went about their daily business: sweeping, washing, ploughing, pig slaughtering. Unwinding long, stiff legs, he walked out upon the hill on a morning when a white mist hung about everything and Nature's sun was coughing and spluttering in an effort to show itself. The people of Shelve, Pennerley and Snailbeach shoved, banged and pelted, the children mischiefed, skittered and guffawed and the animals squeaked, shat and bleated and the Devil began to hear a rhythm in it all – discordant, but a rhythm nevertheless, building, changing, falling out and in again.

"Phish," said the Devil, with a smile that cast an eerie light across the hill. "This is right good and modern too." He clapped his hands against his thighs and a thousand years of sandstone dust flew into the air and alighted on the lungs of those who worked below. The Devil was born in **January** and possesses a huge artistic ego, which is one of the major problems when it comes to dealing with these types. But the morning the music reached the hills, a unique creative flair switched on like a light inside the Devil's head, turning humdrum sounds into an orchestral manoeuvre conducted by an extremely talented artist. The Devil climbed up to the top of the crag and walked along the ridge, looking for somewhere he could sit to compose a masterpiece; a spot from which all the sounds of the surrounding hills and valleys could be heard. Nowhere was quite right, so the Devil began to take one stone at a time from the rough ground and smooth it with massive, calloused hands. As he worked, he wondered how he could tactfully approach his neighbours and ask them if they would be willing to play in an orchestra. Contrary to common belief, the Devil exercises a certain justice in his dealings, for the most part. He doesn't exploit people just because he can, there has to be some other reason. After many hours of smoothing and building, the Devil had made a giant quartzite chair on the toppermost extremity, which he sat down on with a laugh that provoked the collapse of a nearby speculative mine site – thankfully disused. After several more hours, he hit on an idea – he would wander down into the nearby villages, employ brevity and sweetness in his conversations with local people, and assure them that they would receive the same tenderness should they accompany him to the hill to work on his magnum opus.

Two days and two nights later, a mighty storm raged on the Stiperstones hills. Mollie from Pennerley recalled the night:

"There was a huge thumping and the whole hill vibrated. It was like someone was in a terrible temper. Our wise Mum said we was to get down behind the table and wait 'til it went quiet, which we did, crumpled together, scared half to death. In the end, it stopped – a mysterious quiet, as scary as the thunder that went before. Me and my brother Jack were counting: One, two, three...... we counted to nearly two hundred before we did dare to come out – I remember that night like it was yesterday, and so will Jack, I'll bet you."

The Devil sat again in his new chair, but all his joy was gone. His peaceful overtures, punctuated by bright, sparkly conversation, had sadly been overlooked by the undiscerning villagers, who chose to focus instead on his unusual size and conspicuous eyebrows. Then one of the children – Ruth, was it? - happened to notice his horns (were they really that unattractive?) and that set everybody off. First of all, it was just the children who chased him, down through Tankerville, past Bergam and Boat Level and into Stiperstones village. He made it as far as the Stiperstones Inn with alacrity surprising for someone who had lain still for so many eons, and thought he could nip up Perkins Beach before they caught up and saw which way he went. Unfortunately, the little blighters had attracted the attention of a group of miners who had drunk a skinful at a penny a pint. Whether it was for the protection of the children, or just for the sport of it, they joined the chase, shouting obscenities as they went that the Devil didn't admit to teaching them. It was hours later before the men and children were called off by their wives and mothers and returned home coughing and spitting. It was another hour before the Devil stopped running, convinced he was still being pursued, until he came to the realisation that his tail was what he could hear scraping across the whinberry bushes behind him.

And so, he sulked, not unreasonably I think you would agree, and where before there had been peace and softness, now there was fury that split the sky with its energy and struck fear into the hearts of all those promising soloists living in the shadow of the Devil's Chair. But the Devil was born in **December** and doesn't give up if he thinks a project is worthwhile (indeed, he is quite famous for it). He reasoned that if people didn't know that something would be in their interests, they might need to be taught. He drew a flow chart in the dust, which would culminate in the people of Stiperstones coming to terms with his plan. The time line was a little frustrating – it was obviously going to take longer than he initially envisaged – but one thing the Devil has plenty of is time. To summarise, the Devil decided to gather what he needed to make an orchestra bit by bit, in a way that people may not notice and would eventually (in the general scheme of things) come to accept.

Things the Devil needs to make an orchestra

Hearts
Minds
Imaginations
Legs
Arms
Hands
Fingers
Lungs
Mouths
Bottoms
Banging things
Twanging things
Blowing things
Ringing things
Dinging things

There. The Devil drew a curly squiggle under his list and closed the hill for business by frowning a deep mist over the summit. He would seek employment elsewhere, until they had forgotten his unfortunate foray into misguided friendship, and then implement his alternative plan.

Chapter Twelve

In which Time is confused

Time stood on the top of the hill with a look of confusion about his eyes. He had put Story Book Girl in the competent hands of Bear, thinking he would be able to report back to Nature, who would put a call out for a big blue lorry, somewhere Just In Time. But true to form, Story Book Girl had gone too far, Bag Lady had been taken to Pontesbury Gaol and Nature had gone underground, complaining of a headache.

Now Time was on the edge, unsure whether he should try to tackle things on his own, or stall and hope that one of his team would turn up and get things back to normal. The result of his indecision was complete havoc, as Time ran across established zones, creating gridlocks and breaking sequential events, so that everything was out of kilter. Arguments were unsettled, durations changed, and things that should have been over and done with probably wouldn't ever happen. As Time ran up and down, he became entangled with space, until the world resembled some crazy skate park.

Chapter Thirteen

In which the Devil and the Holly King visit the Bog Centre

"Two cups of tea and..." It was always difficult to choose between marble cake and chocolate brownies, all made locally.

"You have one and I'll have the other and we can share."

The Devil looked unconvinced. The volunteers were so busy serving customers, they barely noticed that two of them were stranger than usual.

"We'll bring it to your table," said the nice man, with a smile. Tourist trade at the Bog Centre always picked up when the weather turned for the worse.

The Devil and Mr King amused themselves at the table by playing with the sugar. When the festival had begun to go pear shaped, and the Environmental Agency had turned up to investigate reports of pink 'goo' running into Snailbeach Pool and dazed members of the General Public wandering through the woods, it had been necessary to move to an emergency contingency plan. Once it transpired that no such plan existed, it hadn't taken long for the disc jockey and his entrepreneurial employer, Mr H King, to make themselves scarce.

"So you see, things have got messy – but not in a good way."

"Well, of course I have ideas," said the Devil. "But ideas need to develop, and once someone leaves the hill, it definitely gets more complicated."

"So in your opinion..."

"It's a storm in a teacup, my friend." The Devil broke open a tea bag on his saucer and read the leaves. "You say there's a moose and a mouse and a maid and a man?" He sneered. "It won't be too hard to come up with a plan."

Chapter Fourteen

In which Mouse may be undone

A small, fed up mouse arrived at the top of the Stiperstones hill. He was fed up because he was far from home, it was dusk, and his friend, Shy Mouse, was very far away so he couldn't see him at all. He was fed up because on the way up, he had time to think about his life as a very unusual mouse who lived in a most unusual house with a moose and an eagle, a bag lady and a very sad man. Story Book Girl had gone A.W.O.L. and Bag Lady was implicated. She hardly ever spoke (her mouth being sore and made of paper) and so would find it difficult to clear her name. Mouse was always finding dodgy herbs and remedies in the kitchen cupboards when he was looking for Ray's best cereal. He was careful not to eat them by mistake, suspecting he might turn into something random. Mouse might be a wizard, but he was only on page forty of the 'Dangerous Book for Wizards' and was not quite sure of his ability to turn himself back. Anyway, the long and the short of it was that he felt a little abandoned by his housemates, and a tiny bit cross with his friend and co-wizard, Shy Mouse, and in the middle of this reverie, he tripped and fell to the stony ground.

It seemed only a second later that Mouse heard music and singing, the likes of which he had never heard before. With his ear close to the floor (and probably bleeding, he thought peevishly), it sounded as if it came from another world. Mouse shivered as the sounds of the earth blended eerily with the ethereal and the demonic. He sat up and shook his head, not convinced of his wakefulness, but there it was again, soaring and throbbing atop the hill. He had heard there were festivals in these parts; perhaps he had missed an article in 'Snailbeach and District News', but he thought he would have noticed as he habitually ate the corners off every page. Besides, it did not sound like anything the local Queen tribute band would have come up with. The light was fading up on the hill; he hoped Shy Mouse had got some good shots...

Shy Mouse stood on the turquoise suitcase with the camera to his eye and his mouth wide open. Mouse had dawdled up the hill as Shy Mouse kicked up the dirt around the disgruntled suitcase in a fit of professional pique. He had noticed a change in his friend over the past few months; ever since Mouse, Ray and Moose had got involved with the great Eagle and the strange paper woman they called Bag Lady. Suddenly, Mouse had a family of his own, allbeit a strange one. He had begun to dance in public places and to pretend to be a drunken squirrel.

Then along came Story Book Girl and things got even more complicated. Returning from a walk in Snailbeach, Robin carried the news that Mouse, Moose and Eagle had come home from the old quarry with a woman who changed even as they walked. Her eyes were the colour of leaves and her hair sparked like the embers Robin found in the quarry. Her body was soft, and her arms danced as she sat upon Moose's back. The dress she wore shifted and fell, and sometimes she appeared chilly and sometimes glowed with warmth. Where she walked, dew fell in the shape of footprints and it was rumoured that Marasmius Oreades mushrooms sprang up in that place. The tail which wrapped itself around Snailbeach was that Story Book Girl had been created by man's need for love; that the elements had been harnessed and fused by an unlikely bond of the creatures who recognised the need and entertained the know how. Mouse, with his liking for strange fiction, new-found wizardry and with a little help from Bag Lady, had played a key role in making Story Book Girl come to pass...not just to pass, but to stay for a while. And Ray had wrapped her in his arms...

But something had gone out of kilter and Story Book Girl disappeared. Mouse was very cagey about that bit of the story (the Pontesbury police had turned up and searched the place, but Snailbeachers tend to close ranks when something bad happens and it is rare for any crime apart from fly tipping to be reported in the Snailbeach District News). Mouse had sat around and blown his nose a lot and not looked at the Dangerous Book for Wizards for weeks. Shy Mouse was concerned for the dear friend he had known since they were both scribbles in a notebook. The two of them had weathered a lot of storms together, won a lot of water fights against mighty, feisty female opponents (but not without a smudge to the belly of Shy Mouse, which had really bugged his creator), had tackled and survived the Great Hamster Rising of 2006 (a story for another time). He had coaxed and chivvied and offered unending love and support, and had thought himself to be making progress with his young friend until now, when he looked through the viewfinder on the camera they had constructed together. For at the top of the hill, close to the rocky outcrop named the Devil's Chair, there were shenanigans happening, the likes of which Shy Mouse had never seen before.

It was awesome! At first glance (well it was impossible to glance, without the glance turning head over heels into the puddle of a stare) it was some kind of tower, but sort of upside down and toppling to one side like last night's washing up. It appeared to be unstable, a badly designed piece of architecture that nevertheless stays put. Yet it also possessed a dark, uncomfortable beauty. The impression was that thousands of damaged parts of hundreds of objects had been sewn, nailed, screwed, glued, soldered together to form a sculpture rooted in the depths of the earth, rising hundreds of feet into the air and which could never be repeated. Shy Mouse's gaze climbed upwards, scanning the composition without registering the intricacies. His brain stalled at the point of "What on earth..." His eyes strained to make out the topmost reaches of the tower of weird, and as he adjusted the viewfinder on the tiny camera, he became aware with the periphery of his mind that the structure wasn't fixed at all, but swayed and seethed – almost breathed.

The Devil was born in **September** and is careful about who gets involved with his various projects. He works in mysterious ways to get the details just right before introducing concepts to the world. His Stiperstones Orchestral project had been conceived somewhat hastily, but had been lovingly articulated, with the help of the local people. Here and now, he was the proud architect of a triumphant kinetic sculpture that combined art with life with community with spirituality with music (of a kind). Indubitably, there would be some debate concerning the moral principles behind the work, but the Devil reckoned he could win that one. It seemed that society had firmly based its ideas of progress in the sphere of technology and that an artwork that combined science, technology and achieved a high degree of human misery was highly appropriate to the age.

Of course, the Devil had many items at his disposal and, although his grant applications (signed aka DJ) had been rejected for the most part, he had been able to draw heavily on local resources; so heavily, in fact, that some of the villages that sprawled around Stiperstones had all but vanished. This ensured, however, that he had been able to work without too much disturbance, from his vantage point on the top of the hill.

An artist is said to know when a project is complete. On his return from the Pink Cake Festival, via a very pleasant cup of tea and excellent cake with his acquaintance and former employer, Mr King, the Devil had chosen this autumn afternoon to reflect on that. He had harnessed geothermal energy, using a few items from John's shop in Stiperstones (carefully replacing the windows so as not to wind up his neighbours again), and was adjusting the speed of the turntable at the base of his sculpture when he thought he heard a snivelling noise. At first, he attributed it to the general groan that was emitted whenever he first plugged in and turned on. Some of the more human pieces of his sculpture were less than happy to be there, and the noise of a thousand frightened bottoms at slow speed was not pretty. But the sound he heard with his ancient ears was not a familiar one. His oversized form swayed as he bent low to the ground.

Mouse had grown recently, everyone said so, and Ray had bought him new trousers that covered up his knees, but were cleverly designed with a rivet around a suitably sized hole for his tail. Even so, he was still a mouse, and so was not particularly big. The Devil was born in **June** and suffers from near-sightedness. As he leaned closer to Mouse, his breath was strong enough to blow the tissue from between the pages of Mouse's notebook. Mouse watched part of the tissue float upwards with half an eye, whilst registering the Devil's face inches from his own with the other one and a half.

"Well, well, well, you must be one of the small, furry ones from Snailbeach, who have been messing with things you don't understand!" exclaimed the Devil, scooping Mouse up in his big red hand.

Mouse held his breath. He was feeling timorous at the best of times lately, and an upward travelling bungee jump was not his idea of fun. Added to that, he recognised the Devil from the 'warnings' page in 'The Dangerous Book for Wizards' and never having actually met him before, didn't know if he wanted to, based on the bad press the fellow received.

But the Devil was fascinated by Mouse. There was something about him that provided an instant attraction, an inspiration. Without so much as a howdy doody, he turned round to consider his kinetic sculpture, which was now fairly ripping into life: groans turning into rhythms, prosthetic limbs swinging, farm and mine implements banging, wheelchairs twisting, ruby lips kissing, ruined lungs wheezing, eyes crying, hearts breaking, minds whirring, bottoms farting, and he knew at that moment that there was some essential ingredient missing. With a new tenderness, he put Mouse close to his hot face and with the dexterity of a true artist, ran one of his fingers along the length of a whisker.

"Not so fast, mate, that's my buddy you've got there."

Shy Mouse appeared out of nowhere, complete with a very out of breath turquoise suitcase that had just learned to fly, and a very small movie camera with a magic lens. Through the lens, he could see what Mouse could not: a monstrous living, breathing testament to everything that exists in the hearts, minds and bodies of human beings. As the sculpture climbed, it was distorted by the altered culture and spirituality of the times the parts had been stolen from. Pleasure and pain had mixed and melded over the years, but the artwork was not quite finished and Shy Mouse, who lived among artists, knew something of what it was like to find the final piece in the puzzle; the piece which pushed the project into a new gear and meant that it was finally ready to be released into the world.

But Shy Mouse, who was born in August, was a sincere and devoted friend to Mouse, and having reached the last chapter of 'The Dangerous Book for Wizards' knew that the Devil, who was born in **November**, was brutal and would stop at nothing to achieve his ends. In the limited time the mouse wizard had to study the sculpture, his analysis discovered a miner's lamp high up in the structure. The lamp had been modified to include a small aperture in the outer glass through which light could travel. Fixing his mind to that of the Devil was uncomfortable, but enabled him to tune in to what was going to happen to his buddy if he didn't intervene. Mouse was about to be squeezed through the little hole in the lamp and would immediately become the missing 'TWANG' that would complete the project. Of course, he couldn't tell Mouse any of this because Mouse was tightly clasped in the Devil's big red hand.

Ever since his conception on the first page of a brand new artist's pad belonging to his illustrator, Shy Mouse had had intention running through his pencil lines. He knew the name of everything and he knew what things were capable of. There wasn't much time to play with the details, but he had to try something. Clutching the movie camera in one hand, he dug his heels into the turquoise case, and with a wobble it rose level with the near-sighted eyes of the Devil, who laughed as Shy Mouse paused to get a once in a lifetime shot of the creature we all have within us, but seldom get to know. Then Shy Mouse was off again, further and further up, towards the miner's lamp.

The Devil, confused and with no patience for the little things that get in the way of the big, stomped impetuously back to his art work and searched for the place he had reserved for just such a moment as this. He raised his long arm and Mouse was hoisted into the air until he drew level with the miner's lamp. With the other hand the Devil held the lamp whilst he squeezed the little mouse through the hole in the glass 'PLOP!'

Quick thinking Shy Mouse began a loud cant:

"Welcome the light, lean into the shadow
  Live for the day, embrace tomorrow
  Pass the dark forbidding border
  Take this chance to restore order."

Mouse, who still had no understanding of his predicament, unable to see where he had been tossed to and still dazed from his fall upwards, stood inside the lamp as it began to glow and the suffocating oil fumes closed in upon him like a murderer's hands.

Chapter Fifteen

In which Shy Mouse is undoubtedly a hero

Shy Mouse fought for breath as the air around the Devil's Chair thickened and closed around him like a fist. Torn between fear and curiosity, he understood now why people stand at the epicentre of disasters and capture the moment on film when their lives fall to ruin. He understood that our senses work like machines on standby until they receive signals which flip their switches to high alert, and how those moments of intensity are so intoxicating that we may stay and die rather than run from them.

"Cat Pooh!" gasped Shy Mouse.

Whether as the result of Shy Mouse's spell, Bag Lady's story writing, or possibly Time's confusion as he ran through the hills, the world moved two metres to the left, taking Shy Mouse's heart with it, and the terrible kinetic sculpture began to dismantle. Like a serpent disturbed from its slumbers, it unwound slowly, head rising away from long neck; body lifting away from the deck which turned at low speed for a few seconds, still encumbered by the great weight of humanity it supported. On then to the next stage, as the sky turned black as the Devil's mood, and the shape centred on the rotating deck began to rise around its axis. No longer so very laden, the deck increased its speed; no longer evenly distributed, the gyroscope snagged and moans turned to screams. Sparks flew and the air was filled with the smell of burning flesh as the friction melted, then fused some of the constituent parts; whilst others, dizzy and disoriented, began to pour through space and time. Some crashed almost immediately and were torn to shreds by their unexpected encounter with gravity, whilst lighter pieces (an arm here, a hoopla there) span three hundred and sixty degrees, then flung off in a hundred different directions, each at its own velocity. Then there came moaning, wailing, swearing, laughing sounds – some attached to objects, some free flying, briefly catching upon items wholly inappropriate – a loaf of bread cussing as it was pounded upon by a weeping mouth, a door knob groaning as it swam into a butter churn...

Collecting his heart from a frightened whinberry bush, Shy Mouse who, after all, was not timid as a rule, decided on a course of action. His wizardry exhausted for the moment, he needed to put his body behind this problem. His friend, Mouse, was floating in space (he hoped his spell had sent him somewhere useful) and he had to let people know that something terrible was happening on the Stiperstones hill. Under the cover of the Devil's raging and in danger of being smashed into mouse jam by flying debris, Shy Mouse stood up and began to run.

Now it may seem that it would take the length of a story for a creature of such small stature to reach a village from a hill, but let it be known that, even dragging a turquoise suitcase, a mouse can run about eleven feet per second, which is equivalent to approximately seven point five miles per hour, so the whole thing wasn't a problem in theory. He took the path that crosses behind the Chair and down a steep incline through fields where the sheep are black as moonless nights.

"Snap," went a twig tangled in Shy Mouses's whizzing legs.

Something growled in the undergrowth.

Shy Mouse ran on.

"Plop," went a berry on Shy Mouse's smooth head.

Something snarled in the ferns.

Shy Mouse ran on.

"Squish," went a sheep dropping beneath Shy Mouse's wet feet.

Something barked in the bushes.

Shy Mouse skidded –

And stopped.

"What is that knocking near my house?" barked the young badger who emerged from a hollow in the wet earth and came much too close to Shy Mouse with his stripy face and round black eyes.

"It's me, Badger, running like the wind," replied Shy Mouse, his voice as thin as a reed.

"Are you digging in my sett?" growled Badger, coming into the half-light and blinking at the rain.

"No," replied the exasperated mouse, "I'm a law abiding member of the Mus Musculus family and I haven't even got a spade."

"Someone tried to fill up my door with soil last night – what do you know of the humans around here?" Badger sniffed the air suspiciously.

198

"There are humans who kill badgers for sport, my friend," Shy Mouse began to back away, aware of the possible consequences of seeming rude. "And there are humans who believe that killing badgers will protect their cattle from disease."

"There are also human beings who wear fur coats and believe that a cull of their own kind is desirable. Just where does it stop, eh?" Badger began to feel peckish. "Come and see my nice little den." He wrinkled up his face, either to better see the intruder or in an attempt to look more appealing.

"I haven't got time today, Badger," Shy Mouse squeaked, in a voice which came from the end of his tether, "There's trouble on the hill."

"Well, trouble will always be somewhere," said Badger, philosophical beyond his years, whiskers twitching in counterpoint to the rain that beat upon his nose. He yawned and shrugged, "suit yourself," and turned his back.

Shy Mouse held his breath and began to walk away, holding his friend's suitcase tight to stop it from overtaking him; his heartbeat as loud as the rain. But Badger, being an animal who doesn't like to lose a battle without a lot of noise, wasn't quite at all finished with him.

"Aha! Finders keepers!" he yelped, and scooping Shy Mouse up in his bear big paw, tossed him like a pancake and caught him again, this time in his teeth. Growling under his breath, the young badger swaggered back to his den, carrying his prey and something boxy and hard that hurt his mouth.

Badger sat on guard inside the entrance of his musky, dark home; ferns around the sett preventing even the faintest illumination from the fading light out on the hillside. Shy Mouse sat on the suitcase, approximately where he had been dropped unceremoniously but not hurt; a place he shared with five bored earthworms and a dead sparrow. He peered at his captor through the gloom and wondered how to get out of this fix. True to form, he didn't really believe his game was up and had no intention of ending his days as badger sandwich ingredient. Ever resourceful, he looked around Badger's sett for inspiration and found it under his bottom.

"Badger," he said, "I have something that may be of interest to a handsome chap such as yourself."

Badger purred, rubbed his nose with his paw and leaned forward to listen.

Shy Mouse slid cautiously off the suitcase and, with one eye on Badger, he unzipped the main compartment of the suitcase, careful not to make any sudden moves. The well-worn red fabric cover of the Dangerous Book for Wizards felt comforting in Shy Mouse's paws.

"I was intending to drop by, to show you these wonderful photographs of badgers doing interesting things at night." He pretended to leaf through the book to find a picture to show Badger, but all the while was frantically searching for a spell he had found a few days before whilst mending a bike.

"Grunt," grunted Badger and moved a little closer.

Shy Mouse riffled furiously through the pages. A few more seconds and he would be badger butty meat.

"Dirty cat litter, here it is!" he cried out loud as Badger reached out a paw for the book. Quick as a spring cabbage he began to read the spell.

But Badger was young, not daft. "Give me that book, rat fink," he growled.

Shy Mouse continued to read the spell that would turn earthworms into horses.

"The book – now, vermin!"

That was out of order. Shy Mouse glanced at the worms, who were clearly not horses yet. They glanced back at him in a cheerless, earthwormy sort of way and a couple did that annoying wriggly thing. Shy Mouse's encounter with the Devil had clearly, for the moment anyway, damaged his capacity to do weird stuff with magic. His options were dwindling.

But, ever resourceful, Shy Mouse had another trick in his bag-of-em.

"Here," he cried, and with all his might, hurled the book towards Badger's head. It struck the bigger fellow hard on the jaw, bringing tears to his eyes, and he closed them for a micro-second – which was enough. Shy Mouse grabbed the gaping turquoise suitcase and ran towards the entrance, then up and up he climbed, until he could no longer smell the musk that clung to the surfaces of Badger's sett. Then it was down the hill he ran, little legs flying at breakneck speed across the path of a certain Mr King, who was studying the bus timetable and periodically looking up at the sky as another piece of debris unhooked itself and floated clean away.

Shy Mouse finally whizzed past the upside-down green wellies outside the backdoor and into Coronation Cottages, to break the terrible news of Mouse's disappearance and the catastrophic happenings on Stiperstones hill.

You might think that Fran would be sceptical if Shy Mouse burst in and started wailing hysterically, in a soprano voice, to the effect that they had caused a terrible storm up on the hill and Mouse had been stolen by the Devil after which Mouse had been blown away and this was shortly before a badger had nearly eaten him and then he'd run home and what was he to do now???

But Fran is a storyteller and he had been responsible for sketching Shy Mouse into the world. A friend had once suggested that his drawings might reveal his own character and he had laughed dismissively, but since then he had watched them closely, out the corner of his glasses, just in case they did something interesting. Admittedly, he had no idea that his child would turn out to be quite so adventurous or creative, but none but the most controlling parent would imagine they could predict entirely how their child's story would unfold. He lifted Shy Mouse onto the table to stop him from careering around the kitchen gesticulating wildly, and pushed his spectacles further up his nose.

Ray should know about this, he thought. He hadn't seen much of Ray since the new girl had arrived in the village – in his opinion, Ray quite fancied her, but Fran generally minded his own business unless he was asked.

He searched for 'Moose House' on his phone contact listings and went into the garden to pick up a signal.

"Eagle speaking."

"Um..." Fran hadn't been expecting this. Ray, maybe, Moose, perhaps, but not the blooming great Eagle that hung out with them.

"Is Ray there please?" He felt like a little boy anxiously using the phone for the first time, and encountering his mate's mum on the other end of the line.

There was a pause as Eagle considered what she should say.

Ray had been missing since dinnertime. They had returned from the Inn and Eagle had presumed Moose had collared him for yet another game of computer chess. She had taken to spending time sitting on a step ladder in the kitchen, with one ear to the door into the forbidden place, where Bag Lady **tap tap tapped**, and she had sat there for a while, before going upstairs to her room.

"Eagle!"

Eagle had woken in a flap when Moose had mooed, knocking over several ornaments as she flew onto the landing.

"It's Ray, he's gone!"

When the phone rang, they both thought for a moment that it might be him. When it wasn't, Eagle considered quickly what information she was at liberty to impart. She decided to go for caution."...Ray isn't here. Can I help?"

"Um." Fran was beginning to worry about how he would sound when he recounted Shy Mouse's story. He took a deep breath."Eagle," he began, "I think we have a problem."

Book Three

The Tip of the Tail

If everything is broken into pieces, shattered and spread in a haphazard way across the universe, each of us, and each thing around us, nevertheless remains a particle of the whole. From time to time, as the earth rotates, the relation of the particles to each other shifts with the tides, and it is possible that pieces of the cake will accidently link again. Chance meetings, changes of heart, similarities between people and arguments between close friends, may not be random events...

Chapter One

In which Ray is all at sea

Snailbeach is a watery place. The raindrop curtain is a backcloth to gnarled oaks, elder bushes, firs and ancient hollies. The wet stuff moves under and across the earth, cradled in the arms of hidden streams. Snailbeach is a place of green wellingtons, wet trouser bottoms, pothole puddles and rusty undercarriages.

In one story, Ray, the water carrier, brought the rain with him from the Welsh hills. It took him weeks to gather it in buckets, tin baths and tea cups. Sometimes he worked alone; at others he struck up a conversation with someone kind enough to carry a receptacle for a while. As he walked, the rain spilt, causing floods in Ironbridge, Much Wenlock and Shrewsbury and the partial collapse of the Severn Railway.

When he settled in Snailbeach, Ray tipped some of his rainwater into a tank and rented it out to three goldfish relocating from the Black Country. The fish were good tenants and Ray never quite got the idea of being a landlord, giving back far more in fish food than he ever received in rent. So Ray and his fish became friends, sharing joys, wishes and frustrations. There was a big goldfish with hypnotic black eyes, a very pretty, orangey, middle sized one with a silken tail, and a little grumpy one, who struggled with being a fish at times and then mostly got over it.

Fed up of being supervised, Ray had managed to give Eagle the slip on the walk back from Stiperstones Inn. For a while, he sat on the front doorstep, stroking next door's cat. When he eventually went inside, followed by the curious cat, the hall clock had stopped and Moose House was unusually quiet. Ray went into the lounge where the fire had burned low, and sat down on the sofa. His legs didn't like walking anymore, his head felt wuzzy and his arms heavy. Maybe he needed another one of Bag Lady's remedies. With an effort, he got to his feet and stumbled into the kitchen.

"Moo-oose?" he called.

No answer. Ray picked up a small brown bottle, opened it and squeezed the rubber dropper top. Tipping back his head, he dribbled the humulus lupulus onto his tongue.

"Rye", spoke the pretty middle fish, putting her cupid's mouth to the glass of the fish tank next to where he stood. "Way were theenking way cuud collaborite."

Ray looked around, then bent at the waist and leaned close to the tank, interested for the first time in weeks. From where he stood in the kitchen, he could hear Bag Lady in the forbidden place: 'tap tap tap'. He tried to focus his mind. Were his fish offering him work? Summer was at an end and quite honestly, he could do with the money.

"Wa've bin explooring the concept of relyshonsheeps in a confoined spice," the fish whisperer continued, tiny bubbles escaping her lips and tickling the surface of the water.

Ray sat down on a chair made of peacock feathers and considered the idea. As an artist, he had to be receptive to diverse perspectives... He didn't want to mention finances at this early juncture – perhaps Eagle could do that for him when she got back from the inn.

"Een the dance, we are three red haired beowtees that av been turned into feesh by an Amereecan conglomerate and impreesoned een a tank. We are even forbidden to enter our own castle."

"Mm," he said, hardly making the effort not to sound bored.

The fish continued, waving her tail to regain his attention.

"And you..." She squiggled towards him provocatively, so her pearly scales flashed and gleamed, "You are ower only hope of escape, of leebereyeshon, Rye. Way dance a quartet – I've already worked on the choreographee."

Ray wrinkled his nose, but she second guessed him.

"Of course, weer steel exploreeng posseebileetees and weer always griteful for your arteestic input."

The little grumpy fish spoke for the first time that day. "Ray, come on now, you think you've got troubles, mate, she wants me in a dress, with my figure! Anyhow, it'll be a laff, mate, and we'll get in some bloke time." He flicked his little tail and sent himself in a circle, by mistake. "Budgerigar!" he blustered.

Ray considered the offer. With Story Book Girl missing, he had time on his hands. His body felt neglected and Eagle would sort out a contract soon enough. To dance: that would be good, and maybe he could get a peak at the inside of that castle, not to mention three beautiful redheads at the same time (well, two beauties and a small grumpy male fish in a skirt).

It   all   made   sense   'tap'
It   was   a   wonderful   'tap'   opportunity

Ray took off his shirt.
"Yow dancing then?" checked the pretty fish.
"Yeahyeahyeah," answered Ray.
"Yow heeer that, Flickitt? Wa've got Rye for our piece. What a catch."
"Whoopeee," said Flickitt.

Ray stood upon the peacock feather chair. He wondered briefly about the water temperature, but it would be embarrassing to be caught like this. He tucked the container of fish food under his arm.
"Chance of a loifetoime," the pretty red head encouraged.
Ray took the plunge…

Chapter Two

In which Eagle understands and explains to Moose, who doesn't

Eagle put down the phone and went back to her post on the stepladder outside the forbidden place. She listened again to the 'tap tap tappit' of Bag Lady's computer. For all of the time spent with Ray, Mouse and Moose in the subdued house, she had been sure that her part in the story was far from over. When Story Book Girl disappeared, she suspected, along with everyone else, that Bag Lady had something to do with it. But Eagle had been taught to have great respect for the ability of Nature to heal and restore people and situations, just as she cleaned polluted rivers. It wasn't that the great bird was insensitive, but birds fly until they fall and sing until they can sing no longer. In short, she had always believed things would turn out right in the end and had grown impatient of Mouse's snivelling and Ray's irrevocable fall into depression.

Now, as if she was privy to a code being tapped out in someone else's head, she thought she knew what her part in The Story was to be. She skidded round the kitchen door and flew up the stairs.

"Moose – a word in your ear."

Moose got up stiffly; he had gone to sit upstairs when he had realized it wasn't Ray on the phone. Since the return of Bag Lady, his legs went numb when the door knocked or the phone rang.

"Bag Lady isn't sitting out there writing her memoirs."

"She isn't?" Moose absentmindedly tapped his right antler on the toilet door.

"We're in here!" chorused the Toilet Men in unison.

"No, she isn't, she's jolly well writing The Story, Moose, and we're in it!"

Moose continued to tap – Eagle pecked his ankle.

"Moose, we can't just sit here and hope for a happy conclusion. As the main characters, we have to find Story Book Girl, otherwise what is the point of us being here at all?"

"Aaaagh! But we looked EVERYWHERE." Moose rubbed his ankle in an 'I'm hurt' performance worthy of a footballer.

"Ah yes," said Eagle, "we looked under our noses and behind our ears, but there is a whole world out there we thought could just get on without us. What if Story Book Girl has gone away from Snailbeach – even away from Shropshire?"

Moose considered this unlikely possibility. "Well, if Story Book Girl has really gone that far, perhaps she won't want to come back."

"Moose, sometimes people have to go on journeys, in order to find out about themselves or about the world they live in or even something about the world they have left behind."

Moose glanced towards the room he shared with Eagle, beginning to realise that he ought to listen, to accept, perhaps even to volunteer, although his head hadn't grasped what there was he could do. He had come to love Ray as if an invisible thread connected them. When Ray was low, he would lay his head on the great animal's belly, the warmth of Moose's spirit imbuing a sense of calm; but when it came to Ray's relationship with Story Book Girl, Moose felt confused and had never been sure of what was expected of him. Of late, once the dust had settled following her disappearance, he blushed when he caught himself thinking that they were all better off without the disruption she seemed to have brought with her.

"Ray and Story Book Girl were lovers before they met, Bag Lady saw to that. What lessons could they have to learn?"

"Love and loss have as many levels as the sea." Eagle reached out and brushed his crooked ear gently with her beak. "Nothing is ever as it seemed yesterday, my dear friend, there is always more to discover."

"But Ray stayed here," puzzled Moose.

"And now he has gone." There was no getting away from it; Ray had outwitted her and disappeared without a trace. But think a minute. Had Ray really been entirely with them since the night Story Book Girl left?

"Do you think they are together then?"

"If I knew the story, I would write it down and we could live off the earnings." Eagle spread her wings, almost knocking Moose over as she flew the few feet to the bottom of the stairs.

"But what about me?" Moose stumbled, finally realising that Eagle meant to leave.

"Someone has to stay in Snailbeach. You and Mouse summoned Bag Lady and now you must take responsibility for that. It is up to you to watch and to listen – tuning in to The Story as Bag Lady writes. Mooses are self reliant at times," she winked, "and with a following wind I'll be back by Thursday."

Moose stood at the door to watch Eagle reach towards the sky, massive wings fully extended, proud head sure and purposeful, eyes fixed on the distant horizon, beyond Hope valley, beyond even her own great imagination.

Chapter Three

In which Bird Girl weathers the storm

Bird Girl stood alone and unseeing on the deck of 'Truth', clutching her orange carpetbag. The wings that now grew full and strong from her back felt heavy and she didn't know how to use them. She had learned much from her travels, but her imagination was dimmed by waves of anxiety and cast no light on the vastness of this ocean. The Devil raged upon Stiperstones hill and as he fought the air in his efforts to grab back the prisoners who evaded his terrible grasp, the wind of indecision blew across the boat, throwing it alarmingly from side to side. Shrinking from her own feelings of inadequacy, Bird Girl moved away from the edge and closed her eyes, heart pounding.

In the scary seas of make believe lives a leech which belches bleach upon the pond, taking the purpose away from the dreams of those who swim there.

In the scary seas of make believe lies a slug who eats the future and leaves only slime. Beware. Hide dreams and plans in your carpetbag and do not linger long.

In the scary seas of make believe hang machines that plug themselves into your soul and know more than you do.

Stormy weather
The waters churn relentlessly,
buffeting 'Truth' past enormous peaks of hope and joy,
then plummeting her into valleys
of disappointment and despair.

Her snow white bow slices through
advocaat and egg nog sea.
The sea becomes a deep well of passion, which threatens to engulf the boat.
Sucking the life out of her as Bird Girl struggles to maintain control…

Waking in terror, icy fear stealing all joy, a parched throat stifles the cry of a child. There is no way to cope with this; no strength left, but no sanctuary. The vessel is breaking.

The sea is transformed into a bed of needles and shines with angry radioactive intensity. The fish are sick and dying and mer people huddle in gloomy corners, drinking watery hot chocolate from vending machines.

Going under, notice that Mermaids don't have hair or feet - mermaids don't have hair or feet.

Someone else is here. Someone else is on the boat! No... Bird Girl looks around her, the fine down which covers her body, rising. She hopes it is the Captain, up again to take the helm and lead them to safety, but her intuition and the fear that pins her to the spot, says not.

"Well, isn't this a pretty thing?"

Mr King looks different with wet hair, but there is no mistaking the perfect smile, shiny green suit and impressive muscles.

"How useful my visit to Stiperstones turned out to be, for both of us. What luck to find myself blown here on the wind of your misfortune."

With considerable effort, Bird Girl raises her wings so she is able to stand her ground on the rocking boat.

"Don't you worry your pretty head; I have considerable practical skills, my dear. Fixing things around here should present no real difficulty..." Mr King seductively smooths the soaked grab rail with his hand.

Bird Girl's mind spins back through her encounters with the King of Darkness – his predatory touch, his presumptuous smile. Without knowing who he is, she senses his malevolence and understands for the first time, that it matters what she does next.

Remembering the hypnotic effect of those eyes, she will do her best to avoid them. But now, when she dares look back at him, he is alarmingly close.

"My, my, you are shivering. Whoa, you really have been upset by this awful weather. Well, relax; your little adventure is at an end now. I come from farming stock – a man for all seasons, made stronger by adversity. You, however, my sweet feckless sparrow, are a Story Book Girl – from an outmoded, pathetic, made up world."

"Hisssssssss."

Bird Girl cringes as she feels Mr King's fingers ferreting amongst her wing feathers. Her own long fingernails dig into her palms as she clenches and opens her fists.

When it is time, you will understand.

The energy of the goddess has waited patiently. Looking down at her hands, Bird Girl takes in the cross and the circle, imprinted on her palm by wise Bear, and knows she is strong and no longer paralysed by fear. Making the most of Mr King's lingering fascination with her wings, she seizes the initiative and turns sharply, biting his hand and using the impetus of her turn to draw a wing across the front of her body – Sheesh Kapow!

Mr King is caught off balance by the thump to his chest, but quickly regains composure. "Now, now, my princess." Risking another bite, he attempts to pin her wings to her sides with the weight of his brawny arms. "Oh hokey cokey chokey!"

His golden horn digs into the back of her graceful neck, but Bird Girl is nimble. Twisting out of his reach, she puts her head down and forces her wings backwards, becoming a flying arrow in the stomach of the startled Mr King.

Accustomed to being in control, his recovery is slow and his defence weak. Wrapping him in a clinch with her wings, she works with her feet, kicking, then dragging his legs from under him, keeping her arms up to block his clumsy counter attack and protect her face.

He bends at the waist, expecting to be able to lift her from the ground, but the boat lists sharply and her balance is superior to his.

Standing on one leg, she brings a knee up into his face, s-h-a-t-t-e-r-i-n-g those pearly white teeth; sending him reeling as far away as possible from the awesome power of the bird; across the deck with something like balletic grace and finally into the arms of the sea.

"Tell me what you want."

A voice, clear and insistent, came to her from the side of the log flume boat that rose high out of the water and crashed violently down like a seesaw of bullies. Bird Girl tuned in her senses and peered with eagle sharpness through the clinging mist at a boy with frightened eyes who sat on the edge of the vessel, dark curls separated by the drenching rain. He held a homemade notebook and a colourful felt tip pen and as he looked up at her from beneath impossibly long eyelashes, rainbows dripped from the pen and lit up his face.

"A crew," answered Bird Girl, beating her wings.

She felt unsure of herself before the boy, who seemed so familiar and read her face with a wisdom she thought she recognized.

"What?" He leaned forward and frowned, straining to hear above the sound of booming waves.

219

"A crew," she repeated, using her wings to indicate the ruined boat. She struggled to see through tear filled eyes.

Like an old fashioned doctor, Mouse opened his notebook and leaned close to the soggy page. As he stared, curvy black lines appeared on the paper. He rubbed his eyes and the lines settled into words.

"Blimey," he said loudly, to no-one in particular. He scanned The Story that grew in front of him, and blew his nose on a wet tissue.

"Come with me, lady," he said finally, in a voice copied from television. He stood up and went to her side, humming and gently stroking her arm with his fingertips.

With a respectful salute at the copulating sea, she took the little boy's hand.

Chapter Four

In which Eagle finds her story

Beyond the mountains, Eagle banked left and flew southwest, clutching a broken compass she had found in one of Ray's shoes. The compass told her she was flying northwest even though she wasn't, and soon her body had lost all sense of direction. To her mind there came a poem:

Without shadow of doubt
same as it ever was
precious as a cloudless sky
tumbling acrobatically
through prismic levels
of compressed consciousness...

The poem flew ahead of her, stretching into the distance like a rainbow highway. As she passed each letter, it sighed and dropped its shoulders with the relief of fulfilling its destiny. As rain began to fall, the colours left the letters and ran off into the sky, painting wobbly rainbows with tiny soft brushes. But the letters stayed, proud and strong, holding up the words and making them dance.

Eagle embarks
on a journey of the heart.
Goes where fear burns hot as love's flame.

She flew to Bristol where a man with three children and a long rod laughed, waved and threw her a fish, which she caught in her talons. There were reports of eagles in unusual places. Some mistook her for a kite and some weren't interested at all.

Asking her to dance
in the face of death
they laugh at her reflection
in deep pools of loss.

She flew across Insurmountable Difficulties, which spread like chunky peanut butter across the surface of the continent far below.
She arced above Abscess, Acanthosis Nigricans, Acne, Acrochordon, Alopecia, Angular Cheilitus.
Broke through Beau's Lines, Bedsores, Blepharitis, Blisters
Coasted over Candidiasis, Canker Sore and Cataracts.
She dipped beneath thickening cloud and craned her neck to find a place to land – to rest.
    Following Time's arrow from order to disorder, Eagle reached the Adriatic Sea at night. In this home of myth and legend, she peered down through darkness and heavy ocean mist, which hung dirty drapes across the windows of Hope. A great sea serpent unfolded its heads, rose up and bent under its own great weight, lashing out.

Eagle reeled under the stink of the foul breath it sent to strike a beautiful white ship.

Looking again, Eagle saw not a white ship, but an ordinary little boat that struggled to stay afloat atop the wave made by the giant sea monster. She strained her tired eyes to understand what was happening beneath her. The boat was rocking and rolling violently and the solitary figure on deck crouched low. Turning her attention to the furious sea, Eagle watched as the mighty Hydra waged war, wrapping green tentacles around the beleaguered boat. A ROAR broke the heavens above the place where Eagle hovered. With difficulty she veered towards land to save herself from being swept downwards in the destructive air currents.

Heracles dashed one of the monster's terrible heads after another, causing the sea to rage and swell and the boat to list and sway. The figure on deck surrendered to the impossible power of the storm with eyes tight shut, no longer endeavouring to steer the vessel, which yawed crazily towards jagged rocks along the bay.

BANG! Eagle hit a place without encouragement, comfort or support. She put her heart aside and struggled to fly. Her shoulder ached, her wing bent downwards. Still she reached out, dazed, through the deep pain. Now cold, now hot as a poker, the pain was a mentor, its colour was orange: strength and endurance, September is orange and gold.

Search for her in the desert,
she may lie panting in the diamond sand,
broken there, still, considering your mirage,
needing to be rescued.

Chapter Five

In which Mouse inadvertently learns to fly

Mouse had waited for his breath to stop. All in all, he was a wise mouse for his years and, being very small, had developed a philosophical approach to life. At the Devil's Chair on Stiperstones hill, he had registered his friend's presence in front of him with great joy and had heard his words, though not fully grasping their meaning. When it came to the crunch, he knew Shy Mouse wouldn't let him down and it seemed to be impossible to breathe and less than useless to fight that sense, so Mouse did as his friend's spell told him and leaned into the shadow...

As he did so, the awful kinetic sculpture produced a sound that was a combination of nails on a blackboard and whooping cough. All the elements, the body parts, personalities, problems and pleasures of homo sapiens, that had been taken and abused without leave, by all our devils, began to bid for freedom. As the wind blew about the Shropshire hills, some of the pieces became attached to buildings: a nearby pub called The Miners' Arms is no accident. It would be a long process; the pieces no longer had homes to go to, so they were set loose like dandelion seeds, to discover new meaning and belonging – to find their stories.

As Mouse flew back in his own consciousness, he brushed past hands that wanted to be held and arms that wanted to hug him. He danced and laughed and looked into the eyes of strangers. Eight people, joined by fate and circumstance, flew with Mouse, light as tissues.

The Story of Eight

In another story, eight little figures hung from a ceiling in Camden Market, London. They were made of grass and sticks and were tied with rough string to a reed-covered ring, which moved in the draught. Each figure had a distinctive shape and personality. Small details were picked out by the addition of a yellow broom, a red pot.

Bag Lady ate the free noodles proffered by Chinese stall holders and looked for somewhere to put down her bags and rest her tired arms. She hobbled into a shop, which was stuffed with soft draped silks and alight with the reflections of dichroic earrings, put down her carrier bags and bent her neck backwards to ease the ache there. It was then she saw the tiny people and knew she had to take them with her. She beckoned the shop assistant, who was impatient at having to climb so high. Nevertheless, climb he did, Bag Lady watching him all the time, as he climbed the ladder with a dead man's hand. They didn't exchange a word, she handed him three pounds, as specified on the label wrapped around the match-thin leg of one of the figures; he handed her the little people which she pushed into the bag with the least holes, and the transaction was complete.

Bag Lady had learned that humans establish their territory by adorning it with collected objects. Whenever she stayed in one place for more than a few days, she retrieved the eight little figures made of grass and sticks from her carrier bag and hung it from an empty hook. In this way, she carried the past into the present.

There are many ways to look at the world. Some people use eyes and negotiate around solid objects by estimating distance and time. It can be disturbing for these people when items shift and change shape, and they are likely to be perturbed by unexpected noises. Other people favour ears, tuning in to lyrics, using words and music for advice and delectation. Some people prefer to employ their tactile sense – refusing to believe in anything unless they have physical evidence of its existence. People combine these gifts in an attempt to make sense of the world they inhabit, and the world changes as different interpretations are born. The Eight performers, who had been hired by a strange old lady to work with Ray, were only at a bit of a loss when he failed to turn up at work on Monday. If he had been behaving a little oddly lately, they put it down to 'that girl dumping him'.

Maybe he had just got distracted and would be along later. Maybe they should just wait and see.

Chapter Six

In which Mouse arrives at the Truth

Mouse scratched his curly head and looked around him. Somehow he had held on as the boat seemed certain to capsize and now, after depositing Bird Girl and her precious carpetbag below board, he sat on the deck, seasick and confused. One minute he had been travelling through space and time, surrounded by a strange and wonderful collection of significant others that floated through the air, whooping loudly at the undeniable fact of their liberty, and the next time he had dared to open his eyes, he found himself on board a most unfortunate little boat. He had obviously been through some kind of trauma, but remembered little of it, so it was with a bit of a shock that Mouse checked himself for damage and found himself changed entirely; changed into a nine year old boy.

This would have been enough; Mouse was never a risk taker and found the idea of change disturbing; but as he looked around he had discovered he was not alone on the boat called 'Truth'. He had stared through the rain at the girl who stood in front of him, like the statue of a bird.

First of all, kindly Mouse had registered the distress upon her face, then he had wiped the rain and sea water from his eyes and looked again. Two people, lost and changed by their stories, recognised something familiar in the other.

A chance meeting with someone encountered in another story may be too much for a rational mind. Before we can make sense of the irrational, the moment has past and our chance meeting with an alternative truth is over. But Mouse was a wizard after all, and the words of his friend, Shy Mouse, rattled around in his curly head:

"Welcome the light, lean into the shadow
live for the day, embrace tomorrow
pass the dark forbidding border
take this chance to restore order."

What had Shy Mouse meant? What order must he restore? He knew there would be a clue, if only he could work it out. He opened his notebook and wrote: " ," as he could think of nothing whatsoever.

Chapter Seven

In which The Eight arrive at the Truth in unlikely fashion

"Who are you?"

Eight figures turned their wet faces towards the small boy and answered all at once.

"We'll be the crew. Who are you?"

"Did you come from the sea?" Mouse searched over the side of the boat for sign of a raft big enough for eight.

"The sea, yes, once we went to Brighton."

"But where did you come from this morning?"

"Um, we ate toast and jam for breakfast, and then we came to see."

"How did you get here?"

"I think we got a taxi. Yes, we got a taxi and sooner or later we arrived."

"But who can you be?"

Eight little figures swayed violently aboard the breaking boat and at Moose House, Moose watched as a small wooden hoop swivelled all of its own accord, making its little suspended figures dance.

One looks with eyes like fish, ready to cry. She gets it.

"Aye, aye, aye. I am filled with the rain. My tears will wash the deck. My body is a hug. My expression will move us further than the wind knows."

Two cocks his head to one side and cups his deaf ear.

"I hear the moment the sea hits the shore, the souls of dead sailors, the wishes of fishes. There is so much more to hear than the bold and outspoken."

Three and Four dance to the pitch and sway of the ocean. "We will dance in the weird," they smile and say, and do. Evil cannot wrap itself around souls that are light and dancing.

Eight little figures get on with the business of saving the boat.

Five grapples with sea hooks and fellows. Eyebrows like storm clouds, strong chest and bellows. Fibre, passion and grace.

Six stares into the turquoise eyes of the Sea, takes up a pencil and draws around the circumference of the boat. Then she paints her feet with a yard brush and walks along the pencil line, strengthening the fictitious vessel with her own belief in the improbable.

Eight little figures artistically direct the boat called 'Truth' though hellish waters.

Seven kneels, hands on a wheel, seeing with his ears, feeling unreality. He addresses the air. "Liberty is eaten with a slice of responsibility. If we are to sail our own boat, we must keep her afloat." He issues orders and will be famous for his interview on BBC Radio Shropshire.

Eight little figures.

"Monsters!" shouts Eight, but she doesn't look scared. She skates across the wet boards and rings the ship's bell, then rings it again just for the fun of it, her left thumb raised. The crew gathers round and Eight is amazed. "Monsters out there!" she says, pointing with her mind. "We have to go this way."

Eight.

The Sea raged for days that built the waves into weeks. Van Vorhead dreamed of a life in Snailbeach, with a boy and a moose and a dog. When at last he rose again to captain his boat, Bird Girl was missing and he found a strange crew aboard.

"I know you," proclaimed One, upon the Captain's return, and when he said his name… "Go on wif you, batty old sea dog," she laughed.

"We need to repair Truth!" announced the Captain, thumping the air with his fist.

"Uh?"

Members of the motley crew were sitting at different places on the boat to stop it listing. Van Vorhead was pacing up and down and gesticulating wildly, which didn't at all help the job of steadying the vessel.

"The boat, we need to repair it," he panicked rhetorically.

"Who is we?"

"What?"

"You have a funny way of using the word 'We' when you are getting other people to do your work for you," observed Five.

Van Vorhead did not hear, apparently. "I've 'eard you're 'andy 'arry," he cajoled.

Five looked away with a snarl; he wasn't going to take no cockney compliments.

"Aye aye Cap'n!" Seven, ever keen as horseradish, stood up to salute, miscalculated and saluted Eight, who roared with laughter and saluted back from where she sat with her foot plugging a hole.

Together, the Eight and their captain began to bail out the boat that afternoon. Three had the idea of filling empty wine bottles with sea water and selling them back to the Mer King. The Captain didn't think very much of their chances, but Three struck a hard bargain and Four shook on it. They repaired the holes in a fashion, using the little timber they could find and a lot of imagination.

One inspected the work and tossed her head in disapproval. "Load of rubbish."

The Eight interpreted Van Vorhead's instructions in ways as various as fishes in the sea, so 'Truth' came to look quite different from anything they had ever seen before.

"The mist is see through," Two announced the next morning as he studied the steam rising from the yellow yolk of the boiled egg Three had promised him for breakfast and then somehow produced.

Nobody knew where the hotch potch of food came from, but they willingly ate it and suffered the consequences.

"We must learn to see through the mist and to cope with the unknown," Seven adjoined, stroking his bacon, then dipping his head towards it and tasting the saltiness with his sensitive tongue, as if he hadn't tasted anything for the longest of times.

Van Vorhead sipped yogi detox tea and studied a map of the stars, preoccupied with a new sense of purpose. Vaguely, he remembered he had been with someone else for part of this voyage: a lovely creature with fire in her green eyes. "But hey," he dismissed his own contemplative moment. "Plenty more fish in the sea."

The small, curly headed boy never spoke, but sat and read the words that appeared from nowhere, to land on the pages of his notebook. The Captain often came to sit beside him and looked at him in a peculiar way; the ship's cat watched him from a distance. Occasionally, a member of the crew shook his hand, but the little boy said nothing, for he was busy keeping a secret.

The waves which had battered the boat, flattened and dipped.

"We finish at four," said Eight. "It's nearly time to go."

The Eight were sticklers for routine.

Seven sprang to his feet, hands working at the air. "There is so much to organize! We must bilge the dip, coop the den, fillit the bugny, carrot the pie and all before the waves rise again."

The crew nodded in agreement.

"And then there is what happens next," said Four, jabbing his finger towards Two as if he expected an answer.

"The weather is beautiful," spoke Two, to himself, mostly. "It's almost a shame we have to leave."

"I'm going to my home soon," said Five, dark brows knitting a trail of concern above his eyes.

"And so you shall, and so shall we all," said Seven.

Chapter Eight

In which Story Book Girl mentions something about cows

Story Book Girl slept in the nest that Mouse had made for her at the back of Van Vorhead's wardrobe in the hold of 'Truth'. No-one except Mouse knew where she was and he had almost forgotten. Her feathered hair washed white; her nails grew into talons; and maybe she would still be there but for the intervention of Time. Whilst not always as reliable as people like to think, Time is not one to surrender to forces that may petrify the rest of us. He managed to calm things down on Stiperstones hill simply by moving on, and as the ground eroded by the storm slid and settled, a holly bush in Snailbeach woods tipped sideways and the tenacious spirit of a woman took to the air.

Spreading powerful, white wings, Story Book Girl flew strong and true to land on the rocks. They had anchored 'Truth' close to Ramsey Island, off the Pembrokeshire coast, and she dipped into her orange carpetbag to find out what she knew.

"The cows, you might just catch the cows!" She arrived back on deck, Eagle eyes flashing. "The ancient Greeks saw the constellations of the milky way as a smear of milk across the sky and they believed that individual stars were a vast herd of cattle, shepherded by Capella through the rivers of their milk," she explained to Mouse, and as she spoke, she heard the echo of her own voice from the distant past.

Van Vorhead rubbed his eyes, shook his head and looked away.

"At four o'clock each afternoon, Capella of Ramsey Island rounds up his dairy cows and herds them across the heathland, down a steep incline, and into the sea. They cross to the mainland to be milked and return later in the evening. Follow me quickly and I will show you the milky way."

Home is a beautiful word when it seems we might lose it for ever. For Mouse, it brought to mind the comfy sofa, his own special bed, the sound and image of Moose snorting with laughter at one of his own jokes, squiggels in the cupboards and Ray's garden filled with scent, colour and goodness. It was Mouse then, who spoke loud and clear, so everyone could hear.

"If only we can find something to connect us to home, we might be able to catch hold of it and use it to pull us back."

There was only one bath, and it was made of galvanized tin. It had stood on its end, chained to the wall below deck since Van Vorhead had developed an adversity to water during the first Anglo-Dutch sea war, when an article of his clothing had become tangled in the rigging and he was dragged overboard. He wasn't injured, but there was a high embarrassment factor since he possesses a sensitive, alpha-male ego.

The crew carried the tin bath up on deck and made it ready for its journey. Eight showed them the end of her backless, toeless sandal.

"We have to make holes," she said, "like this one."

As always, they got on with it, no messing. They dug and drilled and hammered and hacked and bent and shaped and painted, then they looked around and found a length of fingerknitting that looked as if it might do. Threading it through the holes in the bath, Eight tied it in tight.

"There!" she said, stepping back to admire their handy work. "Now we can go home."

The bath was as small as a coffin, but as the Captain, ship's cat, crew and a boy called Mouse, climbed aboard, it expanded to fit their huge imaginations.

"Tuck your arms in, mate," Five advised Mouse, who did as he was told, because he was nine years old. He held the notebook in one hand and a wing feather in the other.

Five nodded at Two and Three. Taking hold of the end of the fingerknitting chain and with a lot of 'Whoa –s', they carefully lowered the bath into the sea.

The fish were strikingly beautiful – an eye shattering blend of Silverside, Bogue, Flathead mullet, Greater weever, Mediterranean moray, Small red scorpionfish, Painted comber, Octopus, Sword fish, Smooth-hound, Flying fish, Ocean sun fish and Seastars.

Sure enough, as the clock in the hall at Moose House began to work again and struck an indignant four times, Capella and his dutiful cows arrived where the sky meets the sea, accompanied by two fine ravens. Needing no explanation, the cows bowed submissively and offered their backs.

One by one, the captain, clutching the ship's cat, the crew, and a boy called Mouse, climbed onto the cows.

Mouse turned to Story Book Girl. "Come back with us, Story Book Girl," he whispered. "Stories are all very well, but it's four o'clock and everything you left behind is waiting to live again."

Story Book Girl shook her white feathers and patted Mouse's cow hard upon its rump.

"I can't go back, dear Mouse – my story is not the same as yours. I have been trusted to carry Hope in this tangled carpetbag, but it doesn't belong to me alone. I don't know where my story will take me next, only that I have to follow it. It isn't a case of getting things right, or getting them wrong, but with every moment comes the opportunity to make tiny adjustments.

"Each of us collects our own Truths, and we wouldn't be who we are without them. No matter how many friends we leave behind, and how ever much that hurts, we must turn the page in order to be true to ourselves.

"Our pasts will always be tangled, Mouse, but we are a long way from Snailbeach now. Maybe you will never get back there, but if the doors are still open, you might just be able to slip through before Time moves things on too far."

Mouse didn't argue, because all in all he was a wise little boy. Nodding, he took the tissue she offered him and used it to blow his nose and wipe his eyes, then he waved goodbye to the Story Book Girl and urged his cow onwards into the sea.

239

Chapter Nine

In which Snailbeach freezes and Bag Lady enlists the help of the Snailbeach miners

The air was quiet. Cold climbed onto the back of Night and crept into that special place in the woods above Snailbeach. Ice settled over the fishing pool like a blanket. A lone sheep dog, with blue translucent eyes, carried a stick along the path above the pool, his spittle freezing around the stick as he walked. As he reached the end nearest his way home, his shape was silhouetted against the clear sky. That December evening bit the fingers and toes of young and old alike and they winced, thrust spiky hands in pockets, and hurried home to thaw out in front of log burning chilblain fires. Snow angels, created by the brave and stupid who ignored warnings and ventured out upon the ice, came alive and stroked the surface of the frozen water with their soft white gloves to remove every kink, every imperfection.

Nature had adjusted her medication and was back at the helm. After carrying out a full risk analysis, she had landed the bedraggled Holly King on a beach near Barmouth and set him up in pub management. In return for settling his bail (he was charged with dodgy dealing, endangering the public and environmental damage), she made him swear on his broken teeth to never again consort with the Devil or play live music. Now she shook her head in irritation and drew more intricate webs with every breath, until the whole pool resembled the crinkled, cast off foil of a giant chocolate bar.

So there lay the Snailbeach pool, smiling memories of summer hidden deep within it, frosted oak leaves framing it. Nature turned the light off early and the small animals: voles, squirrels and foxes who lived close to the water, huddled together to protect their anxious little bodies from the deep, bone crushing freeze. The air was quiet.

The morning following the keenest freeze since 1963, a snow angel sits by the side of the pool, poised, still as a heron. His long legs are tucked under him so his feet cross under his backside and his clothes (a T shirt with a winged horse print, a pair of sports trousers and odd socks) are inappropriate for a freezing December morning. The angel, who doesn't know he is an angel, chooses a small stone from the rough track around the pool and pulls his arm back to skim the stone across the ice. He holds his breath and waits to see how far his stone will travel. The sound it makes as it jumps and slides, is like that of a nut hatch pecking an oak tree 'scratatatat-t-t-t--t--tssss'. He breathes again, wipes his strong hands down the back of his trousers and leans further forward to inspect the frost pattern on a winter leaf. His fingers are scarred and each nail has the moon's crest etched at its base. Slowly, he gets to his feet, disturbing a tiny Goldcrest, fidgeting in a pine tree in an effort to keep warm. The Goldcrest reprimands the angel, sawing off the end of a twig with his sharp little voice.

"Sorry," says the angel.

"That's what the last angel said," the bird retorts, but the angel doesn't understand and another frozen twig falls to the ground.

The angel walks slowly onto the ice, testing each step; he doesn't know he can walk on water, much less that in another story, he is a champion ice skater. The toes on his right foot are drawn up inside his sock, like a hoof.

Bag Lady leaves Moose House by the back door.

"If Bag Lady is alone in the forest does she make a sound?"

"Ssh."

Her long ink-black coat brushes the frozen puddles and follows her up the last slippery step into the crisp black grass. Her shoulder aches from writing and as she lifts up the washing line to walk under it, something inside her back tears.

"Keep moving."

She turns right outside the gate and joins the main path, which heads off up the hill, carpeted with pine needles, soft and comforting against her worn out paper soles. She passes the haunted house and waves "Hello" to a friendly knocker who sits atop the cold stone wall. Then she turns right again into the woods, ziggy zagging higher and higher, leaving her breath far behind. "Wait for me," it calls, but she is in too much of a hurry.

She reaches Snailbeach lead mine and looks around for friends she knows will be there.

It is five in the morning and the early shift is ready to descend into 'Old Shaft' as it does every morning. The engine man is raising steam to test the pulleys, before lowering the miners and simultaneously bringing up the men from the night shift. They wait for the signal - quiet, aching, exhausted.

But Bag Lady knows that the seven men who wait to be lowered in the cage that morning will never return to the surface alive. Corrosive mine water has caused hidden damage to the rope wound round a drum and head gear and fastened to seven and a half foot high cages which carry the men to their work. The rope, which looks perfectly intact, is actually so rotten it can no longer hold the weight of cage, chains and men.

At six fifteen, as seven miners to be lowered wait with lighted candles at the bottom of the shaft, seven more will enter the cage, will fall and be crushed to death.

The story happened long ago,
when the hill was full of lead.
But although the names are different here,
their story isn't dead.

And Snailbeach holds its breath each dawn
when folk are a sleepin' still,
as the stories of seven mining men
come trudging up the hill.

Best it is they'll never know
the rope is proper rotten,
but mercy to those who stand below,
the sound is not forgotten.

The rope it cracked and whipped and flew
and near it hit 'the engine' too,
and folk cried out and then stood still,
for there was nothing they could do.

The cage did crash and down sent all,
and in its anger, crushed them small,
and those with candles far below,
they stood and watched their good friends fall.

They broke the cage and dug them out,
and how to tell their kin to pray?
And who to go, and who to say,
"They'll not be coming home today"?

But Snailbeach holds its breath each dawn,
when folk are sleepin' still,
as the stories of seven mining men
come trudging up the hill.

    Bag Lady drew in a huge breath, which crackled like a
flock of birds rising over the hills.
    "Samuel!"

In reality it was barely loud enough to penetrate the darkness of the morning, but the power of magic amplified the call so that everyone around Snailbeach that morning knew something was afoot. The ghost of Samuel Williams laid down his bag and looked at her who had called his name.

"Samuel Williams, I have a job for you and your fellows this morning."

"But, missus, I'm due down in no time."

"Anything heavy as lead will wait."

"We will get sent 'ome."

"No, Samuel Williams, you will never get sent home."

"What's the job, missus?" Sam shifted from one foot to another and his pale face was indistinct in the gloomy morning light that had begun to climb the frozen hill.

"You'll be needing your picks, your hammers and your wits about you. There is a rescue has to happen up at Snailbeach pool, and you are the men to help. I've cleared it with the boss, but we have to hurry now. The water is frozen solid as iron and no boat can sail on it."

"Boat?" checked Sam, looking paler than the lead made him, and glancing over his shoulder to check the whereabouts of his mates. "Lady, there ain't no boats on Snailbeach pool."

"Samuel Williams, you're more obstinate even than your wife grumbles of. Now if you please, and even if you don't, call your men together and hurry them through the woods without further delay. I'll go along up there and see what's what.

"But what do we do when we get there, missus?"

"None of us know what we will do until something bites us on the leg, man. Now off with you."

Bag Lady waved impatiently and turned her back on the struggling man, who fast walked, chuntering and shaking his head anxiously, towards the six who waited for him by the engine house.

Chapter Ten

In which the story circle is complete

There are doors in everything. Eyes are doors, so too are ears. Mouths open and close and things are let in and out that sometimes never ought to be. Sometimes doors are difficult to open, and sometimes the knob falls off. There are doors where we can see them and doors where we can't. Some doors lead into other worlds from which we may never return. Before we open any particular door, we'd better consider what might be on the other side and if we are ready to deal with it.

We opened a door and have been on a journey and now we want to go home, but the journey has changed us all and it may not be possible for everyone to get back.

The snow angel looks up as the miners approach Snailbeach pool. Their breath would freeze on the air, if breath they had, but they have long since ceased to have need of it. Between them, they carry picks and shovels, and the candles in their helmets bring a homely kind of light to the icy woods.

"Excuse me, my angel," says Sam, nice as you like, and the snow angel steps back from the pool to let the seven men pass.

Sam might have had his doubts, but when he is on a job, he gets down to work, and pretty soon the men are hard at it, bringing their picks down upon the ice with a force that is at once ubiquitous and focused upon this particular time and place. They are accustomed to working together and it is not long before they all but forget the strangeness of the task and are singing:

"The ore it clings beneath the earth, the ice upon the ground.
Before the dawn, we break our fast and bring the wagon round.
Come you men, the shift begins, let's leave the light of day.
The work is hard, our tools are keen, so we'll do it anyway."

The ice yields grudgingly, and by lunch time, the miners have fashioned a frozen pier, twelve school rulers across by nine wide and two deep. Bag Lady motions for them to take a break and they make themselves as comfortable as possible at the edge of the tree line.

Snailbeach Coppice lies quiet as a mouse, a symbolic nucleus of Nature's story. There are four hundred species of holly shrub and tree, and in this wood, they grow between the oak trees and offer privacy and shelter to small creatures

248

through the harshest of winters. Their leaves are older than they ever ought to be, and they resist the attempts of Time and Weather to bring about decay. Bag Lady holds a knife made from well-seasoned holly wood - white as snow and hard as maths. She listens.

At four o'clock the taxis arrive: eight smart black cabs, driving up the hill towards Snailbeach. Over the bridge, round the corner and up an even steeper climb towards Lordshill, they go. Past 'view point' and into Snailbeach Coppice. They park up, diesel engines purring, taximeters clocking tariff rate, meter drop, distance and waiting.

"It is time," Bag Lady says simply, and everyone believes her.

There sounds a groan, as the thin ice that has already started to reform around the pier cracks and shifts. The miners get quickly to their feet, more to protest that their work will be spoiled, than to offer any assistance. They run onto the pier and bend to look past the opaque surface into the icy water beneath.

There is nothing to see.

But then there is.

"A bucket," they scoff, disappointed.

"No, wait, something bigger," they shout, as the shape rises slowly through the depths of Snailbeach pool.

"Far bigger." They curse and slap one another on the back in sheer excitement, and cough in the cold.

"A bath!" the shout goes up again, "We've found an owd bath!"

The men swear loudly, but still they stare, and by the minute their story changes and grows. Until -

"A boat!" someone shouts in amazement.

"Pull it up. Pull up the boat!" they demand, looking around for someone to do what they ask.

Then they realise they are men and must do what men will do in a crisis. They go fishing. They go fishing for an empty boat.

The vessel is surprisingly lightweight and rises quickly to the surface. It is painted white and on its side is written the word 'Truth' in bold letters. The miners look for something to hold onto and wonder about the thin, multi-coloured chain of fingerknitting that is wrapped around the hull. They glance at each other and decide to trust that the pier will be strong enough to bear the weight of the boat as they drag her out of the freezing water and onto the ice.

Bag Lady looks on. When she sees the boat is empty, she is reminded of all the mistakes she has ever made and somewhere in her dried up old body a tear forms, which appears in the corner of her left eye. No Story Book Girl then, to come back home and be her daughter; no-one to love, after all. But here is pandemonium and no time to sink into an armchair of regret.

"'Ere - there's cows!" exclaims Samuel Williams. Sure enough, from beneath the water there appears a cow, and sitting on its back a lad of about nine years old. He is a very small, wet boy, holding a feather and a notebook.

"Quick. Help me with 'im."

Jack Roberts hurries to help his friend drag the cow and lift the boy onto the bank. His skin is cold but he's breathing.

"What's your name, lad?" asks Sam, patting his cheek with big, rough hands.

Then "Sam, there's more!" comes the cry, as the men find there is indeed more than barnacles clinging to the backside of each cow emerging from the frozen pool. One, two, three, four, five, six, seven, Eight from Telford, apparently no worse for wear, hold tight to the fingerknitting chain and kick their way closer to edge of the ice.

"Well, I never... in all my days..." muses Matthew Barnett, muscles flexing and straining in the cold air.

It isn't long before everyone is out of the water and shivering on the bank.

Mouse opened his eyes and looked around for someone he might recognise.

"Where's Ray?" asked someone, crouching over the boy.

"Over here!" yelled someone else. "But I think he's..."

"Dead?"

Moose appeared between the trees like a deer on a frosted Christmas card. He had seen Bag Lady leave the house and when nobody came back, panic took hold of him. Not that he had any fondness for Bag Lady, but his life had been turned upside down by the disappearance first of Story Book Girl, followed by Mouse, Eagle and Ray, and it seemed that Bag Lady was the only person who may possibly know how to bring them back.

"Dead?"

It was Bag Lady now who scurried towards the small crowd that surrounded Ray. The cold water had been the undoing of the old sea dog.

"Nothing to be done," said Walter, feeling for any sign of life. "Heart's stopped."

Sam ceased his listening and sat up, ghostly face pale in the early darkness of the winter afternoon.

"Wait a minute there," rasped Bag Lady.

Pushing between the rumps of cows and the lives of ghosts, the world weary old woman did an extraordinary thing. She threw off her long black coat, struggled to lift and remove her tunic, sweating and keening as Cold reached out to freeze her damaged skin. There was no time to concoct potions or to think of fancy magic.

Bag Lady's internal organs were little more than paper, her eyes saw only the blurred corners of things and her brain filled the rest in with the colours that life's experiences bring. But deep inside her body, there lay one small part that had not been ruined by the ravages of time. A heart that has never known true love remains intact and beats as steady as a metronome. The layers of her breast peeled back like the pages of a book, and the pulse of Nature slowed, as Bag Lady took hold of her own heart and wrenched it from its moorings.

"Take it," she breathed, looking towards the trees, and a flock of ravens rose into the air.

She fell to her knees and slumped backwards onto the snow, carving out a snow angel as she fell. The wood held its breath.

Nature was appalled. Bag Lady had made some pretty bad mistakes in her time, but could usually be relied upon to remain, above all, alive. She put on her glasses and looked down at her notes and doodled for a full minute whilst she worked out what to do next. Then Nature took Bag Lady's heart – and gave it to Ray.

The woods exhaled and Ray sat up. There was a commotion as Moose galloped towards his dear friend, and upon skidding to a stop on the ice, planted a huge, sloppy kiss on the top of his head. With characteristic acceptance of the unusual, the Eight climbed into the black taxis, which set off through the snow, back to Telford.

"Moose!" cried Mouse, and Moose looked up, recognising the voice, but not the small boy that ran across the snow to join him. But all in all, Mouse was wise for his age and realised his transformation may take a little explaining.

... and then he remembered his secret.

Mouse had stood on the deck of Truth, with rain and sea water dripping from his eyelashes. He had watched as a great bird fell from the sky towards the boat, landing awkwardly, one wing twisted and useless. Mouse had always been wary of Eagle's sharp beak, but new tears had sprung to his eyes as he understood the heights that true friendship can reach. Eagle had flown ten billion smiles to rescue her friends, and now they must save each other or her effort would have been wasted. He had taken the hand of Story Book Girl and led her below deck, then returned for the injured Eagle. As he sheltered her under a tarpaulin cover, one of her wing feathers, wet and bedraggled, came away in his hand. Poor Eagle, he sobbed, but then he remembered he was a wizard and tucked the feather between the pages of his green and purple notebook.

Mouse stroked the feather he clutched in his hand.

"So, as our story circle closes, Mouse strokes the fluffy feather and utters a spell, till all the ghosts and cows and other creatures look at him in wonder.

Then, all of a sudden, everyone looks towards the white sky, where a beautiful bird is flying ....

...And somewhere, far away, someone laughs."